MURDERS

DOWNTOWN

and

Up North

Two novellas in one book:

Last One Standing

~ ~ ~

Murder and Big Momma

David. Q. Hall

Printed in the United States of America
First Printing 2022
All rights reserved.

ISBN: 978-1-948894-43-2

Tree Shadow Press

www.treeshadowpress.com

DEDICATION

This novella is dedicated to a number of anonymous persons I knew in congregations where I served as their pastor. There were individuals who were diagnosed and treated for depression, for generalized anxiety disorder or some specific phobia, for bipolar disorder, for social anxiety disorder, at least one for schizophrenia, and a considerable number for some form of dementia, such as Alzheimer's. I truly hope that in some small way I was supportive, loving, and part of their experience of healing.

There are so many of them...and us.

ACKNOWLEDGMENTS

My first novella in what I have called my combined murder mystery - mental health/disorder genre was *Cellaring*. The reception and interest on the part of faithful readers of my murder mystery novels, and also coming from others who perhaps had never read any of my previous writing but who were piqued by the concept and subject matter, greatly encouraged me to write a second and third, which I titled *Swarm* and *Death in the Dinner Group*.

Murders Downtown and Up North is two books in one: *Last One Standing* and *Murder and Big Momma*. Each I conceived and wrote as "stand alone" pieces of fiction, but they all share the same passion and deep caring about the mental health crisis/pandemic that has afflicted humanity and will continue to do so.

I sincerely thank and acknowledge everyone who has so generously encouraged the writing and publishing of these books. I wouldn't have done it without your sincere interest and genuine concern.

With sincere gratitude to my beloved wife, also a retired Presbyterian pastor, a former mental health clubhouse specialist, and a servant and helper to a considerable number of homeless people who suffered from severe mental disorders. To my adult daughters who are both Masters of Family Therapy and professionals in addressing mental disorders and other mental health professionals in their work. To them and to others who advised and corrected me when I didn't really write it correctly or with enough sensitivity.

I'm still learning.

LAST

ONE

STANDING

CHAPTER ONE

Ella left Kramer's Skyline Supper Club distraught.

Tears ran down her cheeks, smearing her salon-applied mascara and makeup. Her chest heaved with sobs. She took her keys from the valet, gave him a twenty-dollar tip, and practically fell into the driver's seat. The sobbing wouldn't stop.

The valet tried to ask before she drove off, "Ma'am, are you okay to..."

Before he could get the next word out, she jammed her Italian stiletto-heeled pump down on the accelerator of her silver Porsche 911 Carrera S convertible and sprayed gravel behind her as she swerved out of the restaurant's front drive.

Ella took the first curve she came to on Mulholland Drive entirely too fast. The nimble, quick-handling sports car fish-tailed slightly into the oncoming lane but held the road as she drove recklessly on. The three pink ladies she had consumed before she ate her meager meal were having their effect on her coordination and reactions. But even worse was how hopeless and despairing she felt.

She could hardly breathe under the pressure of the

crushing, soul-sucking stress that was overwhelming her.

A single set of headlights approached her as she sloppily swerved around the next curve. She felt blinded by the glare as the vehicle passed her, its horn blaring at her encroachment into the other driver's lane.

Her Bluetooth buzzed with an incoming call. Not only was Ella in no condition to drive, but she was also in no mental or psychological shape to talk to anyone. Out of shaky reflex more than anything else, her expensively manicured fingertip hit the "answer" button.

It was a familiar voice from her office.

"That's the last straw, Ella, you bitch," the harsh, nasty voice practically screamed into the phone. "You're done in this business. Don't bother showing up at the office tomorrow. Your personal items will be in a box down in the lobby at the security stand. Your pathetic accounts will be divvied up and reassigned first thing in the morning. Don't bother calling. And since you're dropped from this firm, why don't you just drop dead!"

The phone clicked off abruptly.

It was as though her entire life went as black as the night sky and heavy overcast that had blanketed Mulholland Drive.

She failed to make the next curve, crashed through the guard rail, and the already-demolished front-end of the Porsche plummeted down the steep cliffside below.

Ella Brooks was dead before her wrecked sports convertible burst into flame.

CHAPTER TWO

Two months earlier, on a Tuesday morning...

The mandatory Tuesday morning meeting for brokers on initial probation began at 9:00 a.m. as always. Los Angeles Investment Management, LLP, a relatively small, "boutique" brokerage firm, annually hired a handful of new Financial Advisers/investment portfolio managers. They liked to select relatively young people with business degrees or at least solid business experience. They then trained them in "the LAIM Method" of making investment decisions on the trading markets, actively managing clients' investment portfolios, and soliciting new clients' assets for LAIM accounts. It had occurred to the founders and senior partners of the small firm that their initials could easily be distorted into a joke of an acronym - "Lame Method," "lame investments," "lame firm," and so on. But they always assumed a "rise above" attitude about such demeaning, with a lift of their stodgy chins, and a sniff of contempt for any such slur. And it was a death knell for anyone in the firm's employ to repeat audibly such insults.

It was so obvious of a distortion, however, that if they

hadn't before, the new hires for the adviser/broker staff soon realized the joke and whispered it in private. It was hard not to when the mandatory weekly training meetings could easily become "so lame." You had to establish a high degree of trust with the person with whom you repeated the "lame" jokes, however, because if known to the managers and senior partners, it could be met with actual punishments or outright dismissal.

When Manuel "Manny" Taylor, the Assistant Branch Manager, opened the 9:00 session, he announced that according to the printed schedule, "This week you will learn all about the necessary compliance standards you need to maintain in your work here at Los Angeles Investment Management."

Having already put in months of such weekly meetings and training sessions, Ella Brooks leaned toward her friend and colleague, Susan "Suzie" Whitsun, and whispered, "This is going to be so-o lame." Suzie smiled and almost giggled in return, but they both managed to revert quickly to serious, intent expressions as Manny glanced over at the two.

"Now before I turn it over to Maria Ochoa, our Compliance Officer, I have an important announcement to make. In less than three months the mandatory probationary period will be over for the five of you in this probationary training program. I will soon be issuing warning letters to all of you that your continued employment here at LAIM will depend upon fulfilling the following requirements:

• First, you will have to be sure that you reach the minimum benchmarks set for you regarding total dollar value in client accounts for which you are responsible.

• Second, you will have to be sure that your client accounts have generated the minimum dollars in fees, commissions, financial trails recurring regularly, in other words, generating regular revenue for both the firm and yourself. It is not sufficient to hold even millions of dollars of non-revenue generating assets in your clients' accounts. We don't care if there are thousands of shares of corporate stock sitting passively in those accounts if it doesn't mean income for you and LAIM.

   • Third, a reminder that you will have to have averaged at least one paid client's Financial Plan per month at $250.00 per plan. The fee for you to complete the plan book with your client is part of your monthly revenue stream, but it is even more important in that it identifies components needing attention in your clients' financial present and future. And it opens the door for a lot more revenue-producing transactions going forward. You make a bad mistake if you look at this as merely a requirement to 'sell plan books' to people. Look at it as providing a formal process which illustrates for them the importance of planning, identifies the vital need for them to diversify their assets, add insurance protection, take more or less financial risk to meet their goals and dreams, and so on.

   "Finally, each of the five of you is lagging behind in meeting at least one of these benchmarks. Some just a little bit. Take note, bear down, meet, or surpass the goals, and you'll be fine. Some of you are facing a bigger mountain to climb in order to make it and become independent producers in this firm. But buckle down and you can do it.

   "There's a good chance, particularly if you graduated from a highly competitive college or university, that you were similarly challenged early on by a chancellor, a dean, or someone. I remember well that mine told our assembled incoming freshman class, 'Look to your left, then look to your right. It is statistically certain that either one or two of the three of you will not make it when your freshman year concludes.'

"My best guess? The same applies to this little group. Maybe only two or at most three of you five will have an investment professional career here at Los Angeles Investment Management. Feel free to prove me wrong. Like all of this business, it's a tough competition. Maria, they're all yours."

All five - Ella, Suzie, Art, Nancy, and Jack - couldn't help but do just as Manny had said, they looked to their left and to their right with the same thought.

I can make it. But which of these guys won't?

CHAPTER THREE

Manuel Taylor, Assistant Branch Manager
The following Friday...

Manny Taylor was sixty-three years old. He remembered well the day that he had started in the investment brokerage firm business.

Thirty-eight years ago. It's hard to believe. And it's not easy these days. He almost desperately looked forward to retirement in another four years. *There's no pension waiting for me, but Social Security, and my own investment accounts and savings. But the market's been buffeted these past few years, and my net worth isn't what it once was.*

Highly experienced, of course, he had prudently shifted close to half of his investment assets into fixed income bonds, notes, cash derivatives, money market instruments, and specialized income-producing assets. But a sizable portion was in variable rate products like variable preferred stocks, and, well, when prices for those moved up, rates of return moved down.

Bottom line, he wasn't reaping as much cash income these days. And in a down market, the value of his remaining stock portfolio wasn't worth as much if he should liquidate any holdings to produce more cash.

Hannah and I should be okay, but I hope it gets easier in the next few years.

Manny had worked for LAIM for most of his investment professional career. He had been treated well by them and had become a senior broker, promoted to Assistant Branch Manager. But he had reached a ceiling at that point. It was still a family-owned and -led firm, and the Branch Manager for many years was a son of the original founder. The full partners in the limited liability partnership were all related. They liked Manny and his work for them over the years, but, well, he wasn't family. He had gone as far as he could go at LAIM.

Hopefully, I can motivate and guide these newbies to become productive brokers and portfolio managers as they begin their careers.

He turned his attention this morning, however, to the fact that it was options expiration day for the month. For such transactions as covered calls, both for his own clients' accounts and for his personal account, either the options were activated and the stocks involved were called away at the previously contracted price, or they were allowed to expire and the prospective buyers were out the money they had paid to exercise at the contract price of the stock. Again, in a down market, almost all of the optioned stock positions had lost value in the months since the call options had been set up, so they were worth less than the potential buyer would have to pay. There were expirations for almost all of the contracts.

The good news was that the average $1.50 per share that had been collected when the contracts were established a few months ago would be kept by his clients and himself. And they all still had their shares of the stock involved.

The bad news was that while he himself retained his shares of stock, he didn't receive a higher cash value from the buyers of the options. His retained stock did not end up producing a greater cash supply by being sold for a higher price.

Ah, well, I'll adjust. But it would help if the equity markets would go up.

He didn't have to worry about his proteges in the newbie group struggling with the same situation, since they weren't yet qualified to trade options on the Chicago Board of Options Exchange. But neither did the declining stock market give any boost to meeting their value of assets benchmarks to maintain their jobs. And it certainly didn't help with their "prospecting" for additional new clients and their investment assets. He well understood the extreme challenges of attempting to set up "meetings" with prospective clients and somehow convince them to trust a financial advisor/portfolio manager who was new to the business, had little experience, was strained to answer key questions, and in a declining market, to boot.

Most were apt to respond with something like, "Who you trying to kid, kid?" Better to hunker down with what they had and wait out the current investment pain.

And it was this last dynamic that contributed to what would happen.

CHAPTER FOUR

Jack Johnson, the Wall Street veteran
The following Tuesday...

J ack Johnson was a 35-year-old, tall, athletic, extremely genial, and able, African American man. He stood six feet, one inch, was as trim and muscular as he was in his college basketball days as a point guard. He was uniquely qualified to work as a new Financial Adviser and stockbroker at LAIM. He graduated with a degree in finance and business, interned with a Wall Street firm in Manhattan, and was quickly recruited by the Federal Reserve. He worked for the Fed successfully for ten years. In fact, he was the only person at LAIM who had actually worked on Wall Street.

It was primarily for these outstanding qualifications that Mr. McIntosh, the family member who served as President of the board of partners at LAIM, had recruited Jack when he had come to Los Angeles one week to hang out with a friend on the LA Lakers team. McIntosh was young-middle-aged and definitely progressive in his values, politics, and personnel preferences for the firm. He pushed Manny and the Branch Manager to hire minority persons, women as well as men. Manny himself was more "old school" and thought that things like Affirmative Action and women's rights tended to push diversity and gender equality rather too far. But he did like sports and was favorably impressed with Jack Johnson's friendly connection with the Lakers and other athletes. What really mattered to him, however, was whether Jack could land any of those NBA stars as investment clients. So far, he hadn't.

Jack's parents had deliberately named him after his father's lifelong hero, the champion boxer of the same name. Jack Johnson the boxer had become the first African American world heavyweight champion in 1908 and reigned until 1915. It is said that he transcended the boxing world and became part of the culture and the sordid history of racism in the United States. Jack Johnson the financial professional felt honored to bear his name.

The partners at LAIM liked having Jack around. He not only added to their desire to have more racial/ethnic diversity on their staff, they also genuinely hoped that he would broaden the reach of the firm into the more affluent African American community. The managers encouraged him to seek out African American business owners, bank officers, professionals like doctors and lawyers, and of course the professional athletes he seemed to have access to. But leaders in the African American community were like any group of people who had investable money or assets at this particular time. A down, declining financial market did not encourage people to take on new investment risk. It had been slow going for Jack, and no one in his own family or close relatives had any substantial pot of money to give him a boost for establishing new client relationships and accounts.

A further hindrance for Jack was that while his personality was traditionally outgoing, genial, friendly, and gregarious, internally he had in recent years felt ill at ease. In the years following college, while working in Manhattan, he had started feeling out of touch with other people, a vague sense of becoming disconnected with coworkers, casual friends, and even people closer to him like good friends and family. He had never admitted it to anyone, including himself, frankly, but his extrovert personality was mostly an act, superficial and transitory.

He started to believe that much of what other people said to him was not true, coupled with occasionally being convinced that he had heard something that others claimed not to have heard. Such thoughts and feelings made prospecting for new clients and their investment accounts very difficult for him.

On one occasion when he met with an African American branch bank manager and was told by him that he didn't really have any money to invest at that time, Jack couldn't refrain from saying, "I don't believe you." And he was certain that he heard someone else nearby say, "He has lots of money. He runs a bank."

He himself didn't know it, but Jack Johnson was an undiagnosed schizophrenic. His delusional thoughts and sensations, plus his feeling of "disconnect," were milder than a good many schizophrenics. His unrealized symptoms varied in severity from time to time, but gradually were worsening and becoming more frequent. Also, the onset of the mental disorder was a bit later in his life than perhaps the average man afflicted with the disorder - his late twenties-early thirties rather than mid-twenties. But the impairment of his life and work, even his daily functioning, was serious at any age.

And as an additional problem in the office of Los Angeles Investment Management, Jack began to suspect that management and even his "newbie" colleagues were only

12

pretending to like and appreciate him. He felt as though they didn't recognize his outstanding ability. That subtle actions were meant to target him. That Manny's comments about meeting benchmarks, lagging behind, having a mountain to climb, and "bearing down" were directed primarily at him. Within Jack's mind, the metaphor about "look to your left, look to your right" was harassment aimed at *him*. He even began to suspect that his new colleagues were trying to steal his accounts and have them reassigned to them.

As if anyone would do such a thing...

CHAPTER FIVE

Ella Brooks, style and privilege
The same Tuesday...

Ella Brooks was 31 years old, the daughter and granddaughter of a wealthy white family based in Beverly Hills and Malibu. Ella had graduated from the University of Southern California with a degree in art and design. Tall, five feet, nine inches in her expensive designer nylons, classically beautiful with a model's high cheekbones, and always displaying expensive salon-styled wavy blonde hair, she had in fact done some lower-level modeling in her late teens and early twenties.

Her first love, however, had been art, modern and contemporary paintings. She was fascinated by a wide range of such art - from Post-Impressionism to popular, current street artists, "taggers" and other graffiti by famous artists with widely known monikers. For several years she managed a mid-level art gallery on Rodeo Drive and loved hobnobbing with the "cultured" well-to-do that she considered her social set.

In one of the periodic, occasional down periods for selling expensive art, she began looking around for something else highly lucrative to devote herself to. One of her customers from time to time had been the wife of one of the McIntosh partners of LAIM. When she inquired about working for the investment firm, the wife assured her that of course her husband would hire and train her to be a well-compensated broker.

Mr. McIntosh indulged his wife and Ella and took her in as a new, probationary Financial Adviser/stockbroker. She had no particular financial or investment acumen, having left the business aspects of her art gallery work primarily for her office manager and accountant.

Quite the opposite. She had a dismissive attitude about money and the importance of managing its use. Which extended to her perpetual habit of overdrafting her personal checking account, including the one she had set up when joining the staff at LAIM. Maria the Compliance Officer had warned her more than once about the problem and real dangers of her sloppiness, but she jokingly waved it off with comments like "I can be such a scatterbrain. Won't happen again." But it did.

Ella did have two big pluses working for her in the eyes of the managers and partners of LAIM, one solidly concrete, the other at least encouragingly possible. Her doting grandmother had transferred $5 million of investment assets over to Ella's management at the firm. LAIM liked that. The latter was that she *did* have contacts and social relationships with a considerable number of wealthy or very well-to-do socialites who filtered in and out of her art gallery. Her social set had money, lots of it.

What did *not* work in Ella's favor, however, were several hard realities. Even with Manny as her coach and LAIM's risk and investment recommendations, Grandma was disinclined to do much more than stick with what she considered her "tried and true" stock positions and pet

15

companies - even if they still made buggy whips and horse-drawn carriages. Ella was her adviser and portfolio manager in not much more than name and where the accounts were held. Strategic balancing and rebalancing of investment assets held no real appeal for Grandma, even if Ella would have had any particular knowledge and skill in those areas.

The dinosaur-like specifics of Grandma's favorite companies and their common stocks lacked the ability and nimbleness to adjust to the investment challenges of the time. With the declining equity markets, the elderly lady's accounts took on a chart appearance even steeper than the ski-slope jagged line of the down markets. In the months of Ella's tenure, the $5 million value slid into the 4's.

Even that problem could at least have been alleviated if Ella's socializing, partying, social-hugging former girlfriends, and acquaintances had cheerfully brought over substantial accounts from their usual advisers and firms.

Quite to her dismay and disappointment, not very much of that happened. Wealthy investors tend to have strongly set relationships with the people to whom they entrust their investment assets. And those advisers, brokers and firms curry those relationships, maintain frequent contact and interaction with those clients, and work hard to please them. It's their bread and butter. There almost always has to be a genuinely good reason for those wealthy investors to make a major change in where they put their money.

And it almost always has to be something more than "Ella certainly has style and flair. Quite the looker, and fun to be around."

Grandma's accounts with Ella carried her for a number of months in the beginning. Notwithstanding some token and relatively modest business tossed her way by people who knew her and found it hard to say, "No way," she strained to approach total asset value under her management. She could not get close to $6 million. She was scarcely halfway to the mandatory benchmark in her probationary program. Higher level folks at LAIM did not like that.

Ella had always been tongue-in-cheek characterized by Mom, Grandma, and other relatives as "high-strung," "flighty," and a "nervous" child.

The truth of the matter was that if she had ever been diagnosed by a mental health professional, she would undoubtedly have been categorized as having a stress disorder. But any mental health issue - especially a term like mental illness - would have been resisted, denied, and severely rejected by every member of her family.

"The Brooks' do Not have crazies or loonies in their blood." Period. And shame for even thinking such a thing.

As the months passed in her floundering, fledgling new career at Los Angeles Investment Management, Ella handled her glaring difficulties and disappointments the only way she knew how. She dismissively waved them off as mere annoyances like a bounced check. Pushed them down and away in her mind and psyche. Covered them over with her soirees and cocktail parties. Bought more designer labels on Rodeo Drive for her closet. And self-medicated with her favorite pink ladies.

Her work deficiencies and benchmark misses were well known to all at LAIM, including peers, seasoned colleagues, managers, and partners. Hungry, desperate eyes focused on which accounts and assets she had under her name. A merciless operating principle on all levels of Wall Street was that, in the end, it was survival of the fittest. It didn't matter what path you took to get there. Some were *alpha* predators, the others potential prey.

The spoils would go to the last one standing.

CHAPTER SIX

Susan Whitsun, competent business manager
The same Tuesday...

Suzie Whitsun was an attractive hire for the branch manager of LAIM. She had been recruited by a professional headhunter in the investment/finance world when it became known that a young, twenty-nine-year-old, successful assistant manager of a large auto dealership was looking for a new line of work. She did well at the dealership, earning bonuses and promotion after only a few years of quality work. That didn't prevent Suzie from being preyed upon and sexually harassed by two different superiors in the company, including the Head Manager of the dealership.

She was just at average height at five foot, four inches, slim, shiny black hair, and clear, almost-porcelain-like skin. Suzie's mother was Chinese American. Her father was of English ancestry, although his ancestors had been in the United States since pre-Revolutionary War times. She was strongly proud of both her Chinese identity and her Anglo-Saxon ancestry and possessed an almost compulsive drive and work ethic. Her mother's ancestors had been in

California for generations, originally brought over to work in the back- and spirit-breaking labor of pushing the Union Pacific railroad tracks through the Sierra Mountains in the nineteenth century.

She had learned from her ancestors on both sides, and from her parents directly, to work hard, not to expect anything to be given for free, and not to accept failure in her studies, her training, and her job. She must compete and honor her family and her ancestors.

Never lose face.

The only money she brought into the firm was her own frugal savings and a smallish account for her parents. She had to convince them that she could get them a safe, insured, better rate of return than their savings account in their bank. She didn't have relatives or family friends with any substantial investment positions to transfer over to her. She needed to grind it out, prospect meeting by meeting, week by week, day by day for as many hours as she could be out of the office. She needed to amass individual retirement accounts, college funds, medical savings accounts, modest pots of reserves for small businesses and shop owners. She also aimed for accounts for senior citizens who, with their fixed income, depended on their savings to survive in their later years.

She outworked all of her four peers among the probationary brokers almost two-to-one. She neither minded nor resented that necessity. Virtually all of her colleagues in the firm, veteran and low tenure, thought it a waste of time and energy to put in all of the prospecting time and effort, all of the account-opening fuss at her cubicle, the reams of paper to process, for "small fry." And all for an IRA worth a few thousand dollars and a little bit of fee or commission. Even a minimal level of client/account servicing made it...well, stupid.

But Suzie's intense focus was two-fold. Every step along the way she equated her prospects, her clients, their investment assets and small savings accounts with her parents. It wasn't much in the few billion dollars managed by LAIM *in total*, but it was vitally important to *them*! And subsequently of utmost importance to her. Second, it was what she could do.

Failure was not an option.

Her "tortoise wins the race" approach had worked well enough for her to be the closest of the five "newbies" to meeting all of the necessary benchmarks. She was filling her investment ocean one pebble at a time. The one area in which she lagged as the finish line loomed ahead was in producing those comprehensive financial-plan three-ring binders for enough clients. And her problem with that requirement was that she recognized the product for what it was. It served the firm more often than it served many of the clients.

It was really, silently, intended to uncover all of the possible, profitable business opportunities that the firm could exploit. It inventoried all of the assets a prospect or client possessed that the firm could bring in to generate fees or commissions. Properly done and used, it also worked for the client by bringing to light financial needs and opportunities that they might not be thinking of. But at a minimum it became like someone's estate plan. A binder is important if used wisely, but most apt to be stored away and not see the light of day for years, even when circumstances had changed dramatically and updating was vitally needed. And at a minimum on the firm's side, at $250.00 a pop, it covered coffee, goodies, some supplies in the office break room.

Truth be known, if it had been proper and permissible, Suzie might have dug into her own pocket to pay for "The

Plan," as her peers came to call it, especially for small clients for whom the upfront cost was burdensome. But if she could justify it for their sakes and her own integrity, she would bear down and scrape up enough of them to make the benchmark. She must.

During her entire life, a serious stress disorder took its toll. From her high school years through her achievement as an honor student in her business major in California State University, Los Angeles, she pushed herself to excel. In her work at the auto dealership and in all aspects of her life, she strived to be the best. Her Sisyphean devotion to her work for LAIM, and her competition to be the last one standing, exacerbated her mental disorder without her realizing it.

But in some respects, that wasn't Suzie's primary danger. More than one person coveted her assets under management and her accounts, even though the great majority were small or modest. On the one hand you could sniff at them for being timewasters, but on the other hand, she had a point. When push comes to shove, if it was the difference maker in professional and personal survival...you did what you had to.

CHAPTER SEVEN

Arthur Tarrington, young financial whiz
The Training Meeting that Tuesday morning...

"**B**efore beginning our weekly training session," Manny said, "I have two important announcements to make. First, your colleague and mine, an important member of this probationary group, Jack Johnson, cannot be here this morning. I'm authorized to tell you that he has been admitted to Cedars-Sinai Psychiatry & Behavioral Health Clinic through their emergency room last night. And while that's all that I'm authorized to tell you, I'm sure that cards and notes would be appreciated if you choose to send them. Again, that's all that I can say at this point."

Gasps, worried looks side-to-side, and muttered questions and exclamations were expressed by all four of the new brokers present. Manny went on.

"Second, updated performance standings are posted on the office bulletin board. You are all little more than a month and a half away from make-or-break time. I would lift up that Suzie is closest to the 'making it' point. A tribute to her hard work. If you add to your Plans total by just three more, Suzie, you'll survive. It's up to the other three of you to pull up your Assets Under Management and Revenue Generated to benchmark levels. Everyone except Suzie has their Financial Plans up to what's necessary, except for one more needed by Nancy, which I'm sure she'll sell soon.

"Now, 'What You Need to Know about Bond Laddering, Barbells, and Fixed Income Diversification.'"

Ella would have whispered "Gag me with a spoon" if it hadn't been so passe. Instead, she fell back on one of her current favorites. "This is so lame," she said under her breath to Nancy. Like probably a majority of younger, lower-tenured brokers and newbies like them, she saw the equity markets, "hot" stocks, and tech companies on the NASDAQ as where the real action and excitement was. Bonds, notes, preferred stocks, and other instruments considered fixed income were seen as so-o boring, and the many veteran Financial Advisers and brokers who did well with investments like insured, municipal bonds as stodgy and unimaginative. Never mind that among investment assets over the long term, only common stocks and municipal bonds kept clients ahead of the twin terrors of taxes and inflation.

Jack Johnson's best friend in his relatively brief tenure at LAIM was Art Tarrington, the fifth member of their probationary group. Art had volunteered to take any cards and notes with him as he sought to visit Jack in person in the clinic. Art was the youngest member of their group at just twenty-five, a rather recent graduate from USC with a Master's Degree in Business Administration. He had interned while still in school with a discount brokerage for a year. But showing a high-grade point average and better grasp of finance and investment fundamentals than most new graduates, LAIM had recruited him. Art in turn saw more opportunity with LAIM than in peddling index funds and company-promoted stocks and funds at a discount house.

Art was personally "contemporary" in all of his preferences. He dressed his five-foot ten frame in current styles of business suits, paying attention to the little details that made the conservative garb more up to date - lapel width, shoulder taper, pant leg width, even fabric choice. He eschewed the plain color tie as much as possible, especially out of the office going open collar. His imported Italian shoes were the latest design for business wear, as well as his designer label, sleek glasses. He would have preferred to go sockless much of the time, but he knew that would be frowned upon. His hair style was "edgy," just conservative enough not to elicit "get a haircut young man" from the managers and partners while suggesting current styling trends. Up to his aviator, dark prescription sunglasses, "Artie" was cool.

As stylish for a young man as Ella was for the female gender, Art also traveled in an upscale social set. But unlike her, he actually came from a blue-collar, working-class family. He had just discovered, starting in high school, that if he could look the part, talk the talk, bluff his way, and know the right mix of high society behavioral norms and a touch of outrageousness...he could fit in. Except when it came to money and investments.

Oh, Art had a genuine flair for both - a knack for understanding the dynamics and power of money, plus an intelligent knowledge of investment principles - but he didn't really have much of it himself. And he knew that the only way to make "real" money was to start with a lot of it and use it wisely. He saved on expending his limited income by quietly continuing to live at home with his widowed mom, spending much of his own money on his "style" and "brand." But there's the rub. Genuinely moneyed people almost always "smell" when someone is faking it. When someone pushing into their company sports the look but lacks the substance. They may tolerate someone like that, even find them amusing or decent company, but it's a much different matter when it comes to entrusting them with a piece of your fortune.

The consequence was that Art shared some of the same problems that Ella did. He could hang out with money. He could pretend to have it. He could virtually "taste it" as he rubbed elbows with it. But it stayed tantalizingly just out of his reach. There were usually polite, socially acceptable excuses as to why it just wasn't the right time, why investment assets were tied up, why someone couldn't possibly leave their nephew's brokerage, and so on.

A few smallish, fairly insignificant accounts got tossed his way occasionally, also in a polite, "do the young man a favor and look like a good guy," gesture. But much to his frustration, and despite his keen knowledge of investment markets and instruments, Art was lagging behind all of the benchmarks he had to meet. And he *had to* meet them. He had "banked" all of his goals, hopes and dreams on making it in the brokerage business and becoming a rising star at Los Angeles Investment Management.

And he was starting to feel one of his troubling "lows" again. For perhaps a week now his mood, thoughts and feelings had sunk into depression that threatened to become acute and virtually paralyzing. A puzzling, troubling discouragement had seemingly returned from out of nowhere. He had to somehow shake it off and find some way, *any* way, to boost his job performance numbers. *There has to be some way I can add to my accounts and asset levels.*

More than the common mood swings that any person could have, Art's mental roller coaster ride was both extreme and mystifying to him, had he tried to analyze it as he did the financial markets. Just two weeks previous he had been in an exaggerated "up mood," possessing high energy, feeling less need for sleep, rattling off numbers and percentages and trend lines rapid fire, feeling almost euphoric, excited, super-confident. He had been "the life of the party" at a country club dance to which a friend had invited him.

Had Art been introspective enough, he might have asked himself, "What's wrong with me?" And maybe even have tried to do something about it, to seek help, to receive a mental health professional's diagnosis of bipolar disorder, and to receive care, treatment, and medication to ease his problem. As it was, his feeling of depressed desperation went unexamined in any significant way. Only that he had to do *something, anything,* to break the cycle.

He rallied himself enough to collect the cards and notes in the office and headed off to Cedars Sinai Psychiatric Clinic to try to see Jack Johnson. And it occurred to him.

CHAPTER EIGHT

Art visits Jack in the clinic ward...

Art hopped a LA Metro bus from the downtown financial district of Los Angeles that would take him west to where he would have a short walk to the clinic. Like many young urban professionals, Art used buses, rail, mass transit, and walked a lot. He might have used taxis, Uber, Lyft, shared rides, more, but expense was always a concern. He downplayed the transportation issue whenever it might happen to come up among his colleagues, insisting that he was deeply committed to "green energy," reducing carbon emissions, fighting global warming. In fact, he liked to brag that he would soon be laying out a different kind of "green" to purchase a Ferrari. The truth was a budgetary one. Although, it didn't help him with getting out to prospect for possible investment clients in the far-flung Greater Los Angeles area.

When he arrived on the right floor, he inquired at the receptionist's window.

The receptionist said, "Yes, Mr. Johnson is able to see a visitor. One at a time. Briefly. Please wait over there until your name is called."

When his name was called, Art entered the patients'

common area with the attendant and saw Jack seated by a window and a small table.

"Hey, man, how ya doing?" Art's attempt to be cheerful belied the depression he was still struggling with in his mind. He put the little stack of get-well cards and notes down in front of Jack and took a chair opposite him.

Jack's response was pleasant and grateful, but struck Art as subdued, with lower energy than he was used to seeing in Jack. "Thanks for coming, buddy."

The two talked briefly, but the way both were feeling within themselves, the conversation itself was low-key. Art had been cautioned to keep his visit brief, but before he excused himself and got up to leave, he worked up the courage to ask what had been on his mind for hours.

"Jack, they told me I couldn't stay long. Have they told you when you can leave?"

"Yah," Jack said, "so long as the medication doesn't produce a negative reaction and I seem stabilized, I should be back home by sometime on Thursday."

"Great, good," Art said. "And what about back to the office?"

Jack slumped a bit and his brow furrowed. "I'm not really sure. Probably not until I come back here for follow-up. Not this week, I'm sure."

"Well, about your client accounts. Do you want me to help with that? If you approve, I think I could be put on by management as co-adviser with you and contact those people and be of whatever service they need. We could split any commissions or fees 50-50. What ya think?"

Jack hadn't suffered any hallucinations, heard any voices, or suffered from especially disorganized thinking since he had been at the clinic and been cared for and treated. But Art's proposal acted like a trigger, flipping some unknown switch inside his mental processing.

He definitely heard a voice from somewhere saying, "See, told you so. He's trying to steal your accounts. He wants your fees and commissions for himself." And another voice from a different inner direction, "They want you to fail, you know. Wake up 'bro."

Jack began to fidget, his limbs moving almost uncontrollably, and he muttered, "I gotta go, man." But he seemed incapable of getting up and actually going.

Art called with alarm to an attendant nearby. "Something's happening with my friend."

Two attendants rushed over, one going to Jack to try to calm and control him. The other speaking to Art. "You'll have to leave, sir." And he was escorted out.

By the time Art had left the building his mental state had sunk even lower. He missed the bus back. And while slumping on the bus stop bench, he also forgot the appointment he had set with a machine shop owner to talk about setting up a new benefits and retirement program for his thirty employees. He had turned off his cell phone as required in the clinic and in his depressed state neglected to turn it back on. Thus, his alert didn't sound.

But the missed appointment didn't spiral him down as severely as the incident with his colleague and friend Jack. He had really counted on that arrangement to give him the boost he needed so much toward the benchmark's deadline.

Now my only hope is if I can finagle a deal with someone who's making it, like Suzie. No, she's too focused on her own survival and success. He wondered how many schizophrenics ended up committing suicide. *Not that I'd want to wish Jack dead, but it's a tragic fact that if he were to die, his accounts would have to be reassigned. And maybe I could maneuver to get a solid share. If...*

CHAPTER NINE

Nancy Nighthawk, Navajo Native American
Exactly three weeks after the Tuesday meeting
warning about meeting benchmarks...

Nancy Nighthawk had been overlooked, almost invisible to many throughout her life, and usually misidentified. Upon meeting her, people usually assumed that she was Latina, since there were millions of those folks throughout California. When it came to Native American tribes and people, most everyone thought of Arizona, New Mexico, Oklahoma, or one of the other Great Plains states. Or certainly Alaska. Fact of the matter is, California has the largest Native American population of all 50 states, with probably 55-60,000 residing and working in Los Angeles. They were usually used to being invisible and unknown to the larger society.

In Nancy's case, the being overlooked factor was physical as well. She stood only five feet, two inches, and possessed a quiet reserve, often the last to speak in any group setting. Sometimes she said not a word at the Tuesday morning training meeting. If she had admitted it for some reason, she was afraid of saying or doing something that would be wrong. She worried about virtually any situation she found herself in and was anxious in general about whatever might happen in the future.

She was even anxious about revealing much about herself and her background, including her ancestry, to colleagues and friends. She had been born in the Four Corners region on the giant Navajo reservation and Navajo Nation Parks and Recreation in Arizona, New Mexico, Colorado, and Utah. Her father and his father before him had been sheepherders. On the one hand, Nancy was privately proud of her family, her people, and their historical ability to survive in the face of brutal invasion by white America. But she worried about her personal ability to "make it" in the white-dominated business world, specifically the investment and finance world.

Her general anxiety existed for both historical and personal reasons. Beginning in July of 1863, while the Civil War was still raging mostly in the Eastern United States, Christopher "Kit" Carson had set out with his troops from Santa Fe, New Mexico to campaign against the Navajo people. It was a viciously destructive mission that initially resulted in the forced removal of about 8,000 of the Navajo from the Four Corners region to southeastern New Mexico and had killed several of Nancy's ancestors. A famed mountain man before the Civil War, once the beaver trade had dwindled, Kit Carson became a Lt. Colonel in the 1st New Mexico Volunteers. History being written by the conquerors. He became known to generations of mostly white school children later as a "colorful" Western hero. In the collective and personal memories of the Navajo, including Nancy, however, he was a villainous symbol of a hateful white nation that had wanted their land and their extermination.

Beginning with their "release" in January of 1864 and what became known to the Navajo people as The Long

Walk, survivors returned to the Four Corners and reestablished Navajoland, with the exception of traditional homeland in Colorado. And like her people in general, Nancy had learned to blend both traditional and "modern" lifestyles. She attended a mostly white, some Hispanic, university in Los Angeles and graduated with honors and a business degree. She grew to like the great cultural and ethnic diversity in the Greater Los Angeles area, one of the most diverse in the entire nation, and remained there. She made seasonal trips back to the Four Corners and Navajoland - especially to help with lambing season and shearing season and for traditional Navajo holy days - but she quietly loved LA, its culture and comparative wealth.

Her background had been so poverty-stricken and deprived of basic human services, that she felt worried about how good she had it in comparison. By age 22 she had landed an office job assisting the loan manager of a branch bank in Beverly Hills. With a strong work ethic and no hesitancy about tackling the "grunt work" of the manager's office, she had done well, earned performance raises, and within a year became a leading loan officer herself. Her manager had condescendingly regarded her as "cute" and even a tad "exotic." But he grew to respect her sharp intelligence and a knack that she possessed for making customers feel at ease and ready to do business with her.

The primary headhunter for Los Angeles Investment Management came across her name and some tantalizing facts about her business results while scouring public information about successful, young, ambitious executives and salespeople. He liked what he saw - her attractive appearance, her assumed appeal to Hispanic and other ethnic clientele, her success and established relationships with Beverly Hills, Brentwood, and other area affluent people. Plus, he was mandated to find good recruits that would diversify the stodgy, mostly white, old firm.

At age 27 she was lured to LAIM and the Wall Street world. She was excited about the opportunity. But was also worried and anxious about whether she could do it. But that was Nancy. She was undiagnosed, but afflicted with both generalized anxiety disorder and, despite her business successes, occasional surges of social anxiety disorder. She wasn't aware of it herself, but the consequence of the latter was that she did perfectly fine with a business setting where the customers and clientele were "built in." They came to her because they were already bank customers. Having to go out into the larger world and prospect for unrelated business, frankly, trying to entice potential clientele away from wherever they were already putting their money and investment assets, was a whole different animal. The "shearing" skills were much more challenging than with those sheep.

On this particular Tuesday morning, less than two months before the wrap-up of the probationary period for Nancy and the other four "newbies," she was on target with completed, formal Financial Plans done for clients. She only needed two more submitted to Manny, and she had reserved her parents and uncle and aunt for an easier finish. She lagged below targets on both total assets under her management and the fees and commissions they would generate to provide revenue for both her and the firm.

Morning, noon, and night she feared that she couldn't successfully prospect and land the necessary new client relationships and investment accounts to survive. Anxiety was her constant companion, making her teeter on the edge of falling into a depressive state and troubling her sleep.

Rare for her, she was one of the first to speak up at their mandatory meeting and training session.

"Manny, if any one of us is really close to meeting the

benchmarks, is there any possibility of an extension of time past the completion of our program? And if there is, how close would we have to be?"

"To be perfectly honest," Manny said, "in the end result that would be up to senior management and the partners. Like me, they see this in part as a competition. Professional financial and investment services, Wall Street, and the markets, are highly competitive by nature. Live or die. Succeed or fail. Survival of the fittest in a tough business. It sounds uncaring, but that's the way it is.

"I stick with what I've said before. I hope, I want, success for all five of you. Traditionally, again, only one, two, or at most, three, have made it by the conclusion of the probationary program. I'm sure that at least one of you will succeed, and you should bear down even harder in this stretch run to make sure that *you* are the last one standing.

"That said, I have both bad and good news for the four of you. Jack Johnson, as you may know, made it home and seemed to be doing better with good care and treatment. Of course, I'm not at liberty to discuss or answer questions about his diagnosis or ailments. That's up to him if he wants to share any details with you personally.

"The bad news is that at some point he suffered an overdose of his medication, which landed him back in the hospital last weekend. And while we wish him the best possible recovery and outcome, there's no way he can return to his work here at LAIM. He should be able to file for and receive disability benefits.

"The good news for you, is that each of you will receive a limited portion of his current accounts and client relationships assigned to you. The redistribution will be weighted proportionately, with senior brokers in the firm receiving comparatively larger values, down to you probationary people receiving smaller accounts. Likewise, the one of you who has the larger market value under management will receive the largest of the remaining accounts, down to the fourth in ranking who will receive the least. But everyone will receive *something*. It's just that like your own payouts, the better you're doing, the more you're rewarded. Compete to do the most.

"Now, today's training topic is the importance of dividend yield with common stocks, and how it can represent added value for your clients' investment portfolio."

It was expected by everyone but Manny by now. Ella stage-whispered, "Boring-g."

CHAPTER TEN

Happy hour after market close and the end of the work week late Friday afternoon...

The financial markets on Wall Street in Manhattan always closed at 4:00 p.m. Eastern Standard Time. That was 1:00 p.m. Pacific time (PST) in Los Angeles. There were always end-of-the-week tasks to do for the four probationary brokers in the office. Sometimes one or more of them might have a prospect or client meeting on a Friday afternoon, but the end of the work week was often not the most favorable time to schedule appointments and meetings with those potential or established clients. Practically everyone wanted to wrap things up for the week and beat whatever traffic they could to get home.

Nancy, Ella, Art, and Suzie finished paperwork, reviewed trades and orders for the day and week, and straightened up their cubicles for the weekend cleaning crew. They then agreed to gather at City of Angels Bar & Restaurant for drinks and maybe hors d'oeuvres.

Seated around a table for four in the noisy bar section, filled with all kinds of office workers celebrating the beginning of another weekend, the subject quickly turned to

Jack Johnson.

"Wasn't that horrible about poor Jack?" Ella said, trying not to be too loud despite the din of multiple conversations, 'whoops,' and boisterous reactions to a variety of sports events on the television screens arrayed around the bar.

"Does anyone know just how it happened?" Suzie asked.

"Jack has been a good friend to me," Art said. "And in spite of his inner turmoil, it sure doesn't sound like him. He was a starting guard in college, has a friend warming the bench on the Lakers team, and he even plays an occasional pickup game with some of those subs. He's always taken top care of his body and total being. I find it hard to believe that he would be careless about his meds and overdose."

"Really? That's so dope," Ella said more loudly. The other three looked startled at her.

"I mean about his basketball. Hang out with Lakers team members. Really rad." Ella liked to be "cool" when hanging with friends and letting her hair down.

"Focus, Ella," said Susie, "we were talking about Jack's problem and departure from us."

"What if it was a suicide attempt? Deliberate overdose?" Ella gasped, rather too loud in her exclamation.

Typically for her, Nancy tended to be even more reticent, withdrawn, and anxious in crowded social settings. She hadn't spoken to that point, but added, "He wasn't pulling his production up and time is running out."

Ella caught herself and dropped her voice again, bending closer to the other three, and said ominously, "Or what if someone else caused the overdose? Maybe they didn't want to kill him, but make him sick enough to send him back into the hospital, have to leave the firm, and free up his accounts and assets for the taking?"

"Ella, Ella," said Suzie, shaking her head and looking down at the table. "You and your conspiracy theories again.

Have you been binge watching that reality show, *Killing on Wall Street*?"

"Besides," Art said, "who would do that? Are you suggesting that one of us four would try to remove him from the competition to be the last one standing?"

Suzie, who was outstanding with numbers and stats of all kinds, and who knew quite well what each of them had under management, added, "That doesn't make sense, Ella. You know what scraps each of us got once the redistribution was made. Me, I got a whopping three retirement accounts, total not much more than $100,000 in value. Not worth the risk of being discovered and charged with a serious crime. But you have never liked to pay that much attention to risk variables, have you?" She poked tongue-in-cheek at Ella.

"Boring-g," Ella gazed off at the mention.

But what if it made just enough difference to hit the benchmarks? Nancy thought. *Would someone sabotage not only Jack's probationary period and career, but also his mental and physical health...or his life? Am I that desperate?* As anxious as she felt almost all of the time, she *was* desperate.

The thoughts and conversation of the four of them having turned dark, depressing, and even despairing, they quietly, almost simultaneously, gulped down the last drops of their drinks and got up to elbow their way through the dense, almost-rowdy crowd milling around the bar area.

They bid each other goodbye once outside.

"Good luck."

"Hang in there."

"We can do it."

But one silently thought, *At least I can. Yeah, it wasn't a lot, but every bit helps. Now if someone else was out of the picture. Maybe some ones. It is about who's the last one standing. Three to go.*

CHAPTER ELEVEN

Suzie and Nancy huddle
The next Tuesday morning, early, just before the markets open...

Suzie saw Nancy head into the office ladies' room for a needed break before things got busy with the market openings and their training meeting at 9:00. Futures had pointed to another down opening, casting a deeper pall on the trading and investing world. Not at all helpful to financial professionals with major depressive disorder and anxiety disorder, respectively.

There was no one else in the ladies' room, so the two talked at the sinks.

"Looks like another ski slope downward for the Dow and the NASDAQ today," Nancy said glumly, worried about not only her clients' investment accounts but her own professional future.

Suzie was feeling just as down and discouraged. "Yes, I'm afraid so. I spent most of last night poring over the fluctuations of the Asian markets - the Nikkei, the Taiwan TSEC, the Hang Seng, the Shanghai..."

Of course you did, thought Nancy. *Good Lord, is this*

your entire life? No wonder you're leading our little pack. I'm never going to catch up, let alone pass her. Unless something can give me a boost...or slow her down, like to a stop.

"...and multiple pressures downward - slowing GDP's, rising fossil fuel prices with lower production supplies, recessionary threats - are negatively affecting stock prices across the board, impacting the American markets and near-term futures..."

She is a wonder, Nancy continued to think, nod, and almost glaze over as Suzie rattled off a detailed explanation of what was currently happening, what would likely be happening that day yet, what would soon be apt to happen, and projections for down the road markets-wise. *She's encyclopedic. Would make the perfect backroom analyst, projecting, predicting, prophesizing for all of the rest of us in the office. And it would get her out of competing with me for production and survival. There must be some way to take her out of the running.*

"This is great, Suzie," Nancy said, "but time is growing short here before the openings. And more importantly, for us 'til the wrap up of our probationary period. How are you doing with our benchmarks?"

"I'm where I need to be with production - assets under management in my accounts and revenue stream, but those Plans have been tough for me. I'm still two down, and I've brought it up to all of my current clients. Although admittedly probably not with enough conviction and push." She shrugged and set her jaw grimly.

"Well maybe we could help each other out a little. I have one more Financial Plan book submitted to Manny than I really need, Maybe I could get one credited to you, in exchange for some fee-generating small accounts you can afford to transfer over to my name and number. What ya say?"

Suzie furrowed her brow and looked away slightly. "Gee, I don't know. Doesn't seem to me that he would be apt to agree to that. Isn't that, well, I don't know. Maybe a bit dishonest? Not fulfilling our individual requirements on our own? I'm sorry..." she turned back to look with some straining at Nancy. "...I didn't mean to accuse you, that is...well, we better get out there." And she almost scurried out of the ladies' room.

I guess that settles that, Nancy thought. *No help from Suzie's direction. Unless she's somehow out of the picture. Then her accounts would be reassigned like Jack's were.*

It didn't surprise Nancy that the markets and trading day went pretty much as Suzie had analyzed it. *She's good at all of those details.* Some buying "on the dip" occurred in the last hour and a little more, which lessened the pain of the "down" somewhat, bringing at least some positions back up a bit. But all-in-all, not helpful to the probationary group's assets under management values. And not at all helpful to anyone's depression, anxiety, stress level, or "down" cycle in a bipolar disorder.

The Tuesday morning training meeting had been pretty routine, the main topic covered by Manny had been "Diversification by the Use of Cash Equivalents."

Per usual, Ella had been in the advanced stages of utter boredom. Fact of the matter was, if it wasn't "This Is Your Next Secret Hot Stock," she wasn't going to be much enthused.

Nancy and Suzie had been left with a little brooding uneasiness following their pre-training meeting conversation in the ladies' room.

Only Art seemed "up," even more energized and "eager to go" than usual. Having absolutely no idea why or how, his mental and psychological cycle had surprisingly swung up over the previous weekend. Again, being undiagnosed or treated, he didn't really know that he had entered a manic episode of his bipolar disorder. All he knew was that his mood had elevated. He didn't need as much sleep. His thinking was "on fire," full of exciting ideas. And, his sense of self-esteem had returned to being much more positive. He still lagged short in each of the three required benchmarks of investment total book value, revenue generated, and those pesky Financial Plan books. But somehow, he was convinced he could still do it in the next month and a half.

Especially if I can get a little help, and my competition slacks off.

Or somehow is gone.

CHAPTER TWELVE

Another probationary broker out of the running.
Late Friday afternoon of the following week, just
a month to go...

Still in his manic phase from the last two weeks, Arthur Tarrington's current episode was capable of lasting for weeks, a month or more. His euphoric self-confidence had soared well beyond the hard realities of his prospects of success in his probationary period. He had only picked up one more client account relationship in the previous two weeks. It included a young physician's modest stock portfolio in a standard retail account, his comparatively new IRA, and a joint checking account with the young doctor's spouse as secondary on the account. It added a few thousand dollars to his total asset values, but there was not a lot of near-term potential for more as the physician had to pour a substantial portion of monthly income into student loan repayment.

Nonetheless, Art was so sure of himself that after leaving the LAIM office for that week, an office colleague accompanied him to do a "little window-shopping" on Rodeo Drive in Beverly Hills. They popped in and out of several stores - an upscale men's clothing store that featured expensive Italian suits, shoes and accessories, an art boutique, and finally a high-end jewelry store. Art had especially been attracted to a display of expensive Rolex men's watches.

They went inside, lingered at the display case featuring the fancy watches. Before long, an excessively smiling clerk came over to offer assistance.

"Would sir like to try one on? Which one particularly appeals to your fine sense of taste?"

Despite his euphoric feelings and his exaggerated sense of well-being, Art hesitated at the price tags. He had been focused on a glittering Cosmograph Daytona, Oystersteel, and 18 ct. yellow gold, black dial, engraved tachymetric scale, at $17,400.

"Go on, try it on your wrist. You'll love it. It's the right choice for a young urban professional like yourself. Perfect complement to your Giorgio Armani sharkskin suit."

The suave clerk knew his high-end products. Never mind that the watch was priced at over five times the cost of what was frankly an expensive suit. But he had hooked Art's interest with the words, "right choice for a young urban professional like yourself." One of the regrettable symptoms of a manic phase of bipolar can be poor decision-making and reckless shopping sprees.

"Why don't you walk around the counters a little bit? You'll notice how it feels on your wrist as you move, and how the ladies glance at such a finely-jeweled chronograph...and you, of course. Just don't leave the store until we've wrapped it up for you," He winked and smiled, but obviously tucked into his casual, polite words was a definite warning. "I just have to speak to our employee over here for a second while you pick out what else you'd like to complement such a wise choice."

Art took the clerk's advice, sauntering casually around a center glass-topped display case, lifting his left wrist a couple of times to admire the Rolex. *It does feel good. And my business success should rise to be able to handle the payments. I should definitely consider this.*

The clerk was engaged in a quiet conversation with the store security guard about occupancy limits on the number of customers allowed in the shop at any one time. But he kept glancing in Art's direction in his slow walk around.

But as Art rounded the end of the center display case that was closest to the main door, his colleague from the office, walking close behind him, leaned close and whispered in an urgent tone in Art's ear.

"He's telling that security guard that you're trying to steal that Rolex and take it out the door. Quick, run, and shed the watch!" But Art's office friend stayed put.

Other difficult symptoms of bipolar disorder mania include being easily distracted, racing thoughts and feelings, impulsive actions, and of course, those poor decisions.

Art panicked.

He raced toward the door, fumbling with the clasp of the watch as he went. He managed to toss it down onto the carpeted floor just as he exited, and literally ran for his life out to the street corner where there was a Metro Bus Stop.

He never saw the bus that was pulling up to the stop.

One of the reasons that phrases like "being run over by a bus" become generic examples of personal misfortune, even cliches and jokes, is that occasionally it actually happens. And in the case of being hit by a proverbial bus, it actually happens to someone far more often than dying in a plane crash.

Ironically and tragically, the same mode of transportation that Art had so often depended upon to get around the LA area was the cause of his death.

The next day, Saturday, his client relationships and accounts were regrettably reassigned around the office as Jack's had been.

Well, regrettable to some.

CHAPTER THIRTEEN

*The Training Meeting becomes a time of
mourning
The following Tuesday morning...*

The three probationary brokers and portfolio managers had already been distressed about the circumstances of Jack Johnson and his schizophrenia and near-fatal overdose. Now they mourned the assuredly accidental death of Art Tarrington. Suzie, Ella, and Nancy realized that their competition to complete the program and become full, independent Financial Advisers and investment managers had suddenly been reduced by forty per cent. But the first emotion for all three was grief and loss. Although Ella soon wondered how many accounts and of what value she would receive from Art's book of clients.

LAIM management, including Manny, realized that one of their primary goals of adding more diversification to their team had now suffered the loss of their only African American broker and both of the young men in the probationary group. On the other hand, the three young women were still "live" in this last month of their program, and one was Chinese American, with one being the firm's first Native American.

Besides, historical statistics almost guaranteed that out of the original group of five, at most two, rarely three, would survive the program by meeting all of the benchmarks. And it wasn't uncommon each year for only one to be the last one standing. One of the McIntosh founding family partners, an avid Nature advocate and board member of the Los Angeles Zoo & Botanical Gardens, in a bit of dark humor was fond of referring to the sole survivor, if it went that way, as "the endling." The last member of its species.

"It's just so bogus," Ella said to Suzie and Nancy. "I mean, yah, they were competing with us to make it here at 'Lame' company, but nobody wanted them to be taken out by mental illness and death. Fubar, you know?" Ella had never served in any branch of the U.S. military, but she liked that historical slang among soldiers and marines for "unbelievably messed up."

Well, maybe not "nobody." Nancy mulled silently. *I wonder.*

Ella pivoted quickly from her few seconds of mournful expression and reverted to her constant stress of still not fulfilling any and all of the benchmark requirements.

"Shit," she couldn't restrain herself even in the professional setting of their training room. "I really need those reassigned accounts from Art. Have either of you heard? Will Manny pass out assignment lists this morning?"

Ella was by nature more social, more verbal, more uninhibited, in her personality and behavior than her two comparatively quieter peers. She was also, as her mother and other family members had put it, more "high-strung." Stressed. Suzie was more apt to open up and verbalize when the subjects turned to financial markets, numbers, graphs, trend lines, the blizzard of hard data and statistics in the world of finance and investing. Nancy was almost always worried and felt anxious about anything she might say or reveal.

"I haven't heard or seen anything in our mailboxes," Suzie said. Ella often forgot to check her mailbox in the array outside the mail room in the hallway. Or she casually avoided bothering with the clutter of announcements, warnings from Compliance, including annoying overdraft memos, "promo" sheets for the mutual fund "flavor of the month," and all of the other circular file papers.

Nancy merely shook her head and said, "Nope," and "Dunno."

Manny walked in, greeted the three, and proceeded to make appropriate comments of condolences and regret at the tragic passing of Art in such a bizarre accident. He gave no update or additional information about Jack. It was not unusual in the fast-moving and constantly merciless world of the financial and investing industry for even prominent persons, their names and reputations, to be left behind quickly and seem to be past, gone, and forgotten. And past achievements and glory vanished under the crushing reality of "What have you done lately, today, and will do tomorrow?" Sentimentality and lingering found no refuge on the trading floors of Wall Street and Chicago.

He did share, however, that a memorial service for Art would be held Friday afternoon of that week, 4:00 p.m., at the City of Angels Pentecostal Tabernacle in West Hills. It would be followed by interment in the church's Memorial Garden, then a reception with light refreshments back at the church hall. The comparative lateness of the arrangements on a Friday afternoon was a little unusual, but the family was at the mercy of a busy schedule at the mortuary, the availability of space at the church, and everyone else's schedules. After all, Angelenos, even a good number of relatives in Art's family, had to finish up their work week at their respective offices and businesses. Even death and burial could just chill out until other demands were met.

"Two quick announcements," Manny began. "First, I'm sure the three of you are aware that we're only three weeks away from your finish line in this probationary program. Quick tally: Suzie has made it at this point in terms of revenue brought in. That's set. You're pretty close on total value of assets in your client accounts, not that the market declines have helped anyone. A strong finishing kick down the stretch should enable you to break that tape and cross the line. Bear down and keep prospecting. But still two plans short. My advice, get one done each of these next two weeks, then you can breathe as you finish the last week.

"Ella, you only need one Financial Plan handed in. You can find someone to do that for. Investment assets value and secured revenue are another story. It would behoove you to land a really good new client relationship in these final weeks, big enough to carry you across the finish line.

"And Nancy, congratulations on more than enough plan books turned in. But as you know, still coming up short on account values and set revenue for this month and totaling for the entire program period. Strong finishing kick, everyone. Strong finishing kick!" Obviously, track and field was the chosen metaphorical setting for the day.

"And my second announcement. I'm available this week, and this week only, to accompany any or all of you if you want backup or assistance in sealing the deal with any strong prospect. Don't waste my time and yours tag-teaming a $5,000 retirement account that won't get it done for you. But sometimes with an "elephant" of a prospect target, it can both favorably impress, and get the signatures, to have a senior management member of their soon-to-be new investment firm meeting them face-to-face. Together we'll land that white whale."

Apparently, it was also a morning for mixed metaphors. It was a long-standing, traditional metaphor to refer to bigger, more valuable, prospective new clients as "elephants." And a truism edging into cliche-world was that in order to bag elephants, you had to go where the elephants are. Although the truism was a little less commonly used these days with more widespread concern about the tragic, terrible slaughter of wild elephants throughout Africa and Asia. "White whale" was obvious. Unless omitted in the less literate education of more recent times.

But Ella had recently spotted her elephant, or her white whale, or, more plainly, the prospect that could secure her success. And Manny's offer could raise her up to that elusive success level that had so long evaded her.

"Now," Manny transitioned to their training subject and material for the morning. "All that you need and so desperately want to know about annuities and other insurance products. How they can supplement your clients' longer-term financial futures."

Suzie perked up at the prospect of even more numbers, actuarial tables, guaranteed rates of return, annuitized payouts and all such details.

Nancy's thoughts diverted to the usual inability of her family and people back at Four Corners country even to afford insurance premiums or purchase an annuity.

It was all Ella could do not to groan and pass out. *Whatever happens to me here in Lameland, I'll be so-o glad when these Tuesday mornings are over.*

And when the morning's session *was* finally over, Ella rallied and asked to talk to Manny privately.

"I have an opportunity to make a proposal to a major Hollywood producer this coming Friday evening. How 'bout you come along, if you're available, after Art's memorial service. We can be out of that West Hills church, say 7:00.

I'm going to meet this guy at Kramer's Skyline Supper Club on Mulholland Drive at 8:00, cocktails and light entrees. You know, the little filet mignon medallions they serve there with a little dab of this, a sprig of that. A man of his stature and net worth, he'll be more impressed if I'm backed up by a senior broker. We can pitch as a team."

"I could be available," Manny said. "I need to be at that service and reception anyway. Tell me something about this fellow. How did you make the contact? And what do you plan to propose? Did you obtain any statements from him of current holdings in his investment portfolio to know what better strategy or positions to recommend? The more I know going in, the better I can help."

"Okay, well, it's actually my dad who knows him. His name is Armstrong. They met at a dinner last year, before I started with Los Angeles Investment Management, and my mom and I were along. He and Dad have talked about work on sets in one or more of his productions, and one time recently he said he remembered me and spoke well of me. Dad told him that I'm working here now, and could I contact him? He said, sure, tell her to call me. So that's how I landed the meeting."

"Doesn't sound like a lot of relationship to take advantage of," Manny said, "but the important thing is you're getting in front of him, and getting the meeting is the essential first step, so we'll work with what we have. And any recent investment statements?"

"Ah, well, no, but he said we could get to that after a comfort level is established. I didn't want to push him prematurely, you know, scare him off."

"Well," Manny furrowed his brow. "It's hard to make any specific proposals or recommendations to improve his investment growth, returns, income stream, whatever his hopes and dreams are, without knowing where we're starting. We'll have to emphasize investment philosophy, the history, and principles of our firm. Ask some questions concerning his attitudes about risk. What is the end result he wants to accomplish with his money? Is it a more prosperous retirement lifestyle? Any children or grandchildren heading off to college down the road? More current income to supplement whatever his needs are right now? That South Sea island he's always wanted? Reserves to plow into his producing work? What does he really want?

"A really specific proposal may have to wait until we get that kind of vital information. And those current statements. But I well understand that you need transfer papers signed by him right now for successful completion of your probationary requirements. We can do this for you. If you manage to secure at least verbal commitment, followed up quickly with signed papers, you can probably get tentative credit in your favor before the accounts actually come over to us."

"Well," Ella said, "he *did* indicate a lot of liquidity available, that he likes to keep a substantial sum in cash, in order respond to needs as soon as they arise, not hold up anything in his work."

Manny smiled at that revelation. "That would be ideal, of course. If he would sign up with you and was able to write a big check for money in his bank, or even better, make a large initial deposit with a bank check, cashier's or certified, then you would have the dollar value in his new account or accounts with you. And you wouldn't even have to worry about stock positions or mutual funds that are declining in market value as you wait to transfer them in.

"Okay, let's see if we can bag that elephant, harpoon that whale. Memorial service, then be at Kramer's by 7:50. Never keep a client or prospect waiting. Plan to arrive before they do."

Manny was too old school to possess much sensitivity about extinction threats for the world's wild elephants, let alone the serious decline of whale populations in the oceans. But they had a plan.

CHAPTER FOURTEEN

The Prospect meeting at Kramer's
After Art's memorial service, exactly two weeks
to go to end of probation...

Ella and Manny drove separately up to Kramer's Skyline Supper Club. Once their meeting with Ella's "elephant"/white whale concluded, they would take their own cars home in different directions. Besides, Manny wasn't about to be alone with a beautiful, stylish, young subordinate of the opposite gender. Not only were the professional guidelines and policies very clear about that, but he also personally abhorred any sexual element in the office, their working relationships, and particularly in his own life and work. He had never even flirted with anyone at work. Not only was he happily married, but he also considered himself something of a "puritan" when it came to sex.

Ella got there first, deciding that it would be prudent to arrive not only before her prospect, but also before her boss. It was almost 7:45. Manny arrived at exactly 7:50, as he had recommended. He noted with small approval that Ella had gotten there before him. Their white whale didn't wander into the reception area until about 8:18.

Jay Armstrong frequently went with "stylishly late." It was a common Hollywood practice to "make an entrance," almost casually assuming privilege, intentionally waiting for the crowd to assemble to await the person of importance.

"Mr. Armstrong," Ella flashed her well-trained, best smile. "So glad to see you again. I'd like to introduce you to my colleague Manuel Taylor, one of the most senior of the investment professionals at Los Angeles Investment Management. He will partner with me for this initial meeting and provide a tremendous resource as we begin discussing a more prosperous present and future for you."

Jay was a large man in his sixties. He was six feet tall but weighed in the vicinity of 250 pounds. He liked to sport a rather shaggy mane of gray-black hair, deliberately projecting a swinging, slightly "wild" look that was actually shaped and maintained by an expensive, exclusive salon. He had come in a French open collar silk shirt, displaying a heavy, woven 18-carat gold necklace, and a diamond stud in his ear lobe. He exhibited an "edgy" style, but expected to be regarded as a serious businessman of the upper class.

He looked at Ella first, smiled widely, then turned his head toward Manny, changing his expression to one of curiosity, if not perplexity. The beginning of this meeting was not just what he expected. Manny and he exchanged greetings and a handshake, and the maître d' invited them to follow him to their reserved table.

"Please, lead our way," Jay said to Manny, smiling more broadly this time. So, Manny followed the maître d' with Ella and Jay coming behind. Jay leaned close to Ella.

"I thought this was going to be the two of us."

Ella repeated what she had said in her introduction a moment ago. "You'll find Mr. Taylor to be a helpful addition to our discussion tonight. He's extremely experienced, knowledgeable, and successful with our clients like yourself." It seemed to her as though Jay replied with a "humph."

Their cocktails went okay, but with Jay becoming more expansive and louder about his big productions as the first whiskey sour gave way to the second, then the third. Both Ella and Manny kept trying to focus their conversation on investing matters and what LAIM could do for a man like Jay Armstrong. But while he would pretend interest at points, both had an unspoken feeling that he was being dismissive about what they were sharing.

Once while finishing his second drink, Jay actually said, "You know, we have plenty of time and opportunity to get into all of that next time."

Manny also noticed that as the drinks proceeded, Jay seemed to swing his attention increasingly in Ella's direction. At another moment Manny made a pertinent point about the very active, regular rebalancing of assets that their firm would conscientiously conduct for Jay's portfolio.

"We're not just passive holders of your accounts, but work with you all the time for your benefit. And we manage your risk exposure to fit your comfort level and goals."

To which Jay responded by taking a big sip of his whiskey sour, winking at Ella, and saying, "I'd like to hear more about that holding part. And my benefit. And comfort."

Ella was glad that he didn't include a reference to "exposure."

As both Jay and Ella were finishing their third drinks, Manny excused himself and headed for the men's room, shaking his head and muttering to himself. After a few minutes he returned and was stunned at what he saw.

As soon as Manny was out of sight of their table, Jay inched closer to Ella and started whispering to her.

"You know, you didn't have to bring Grandpa with you. You and I could have a lot of fun if you ditched him. Besides, I want to conduct my business with you, not with the old fuddy-duddy. Your daddy always said what a fun girl you are."

Ella was greatly confused about what was happening to their meeting. To her. The whole situation ratcheted up her stress feelings. On the one hand she was sickened by the blatant way he was coming on to her. He was old enough to be her father and then some. On the other hand, she desperately needed his investment accounts and bankroll. She was totally unprepared, though, for what happened next.

"Lean a little closer, Ella, and I'll tell you, and just you, how you can get my business."

And then he suddenly put a hand behind her head, pulled her even closer, and kissed her on her lips. Ella frantically put a hand on his shoulder to push him away, but at that precise moment Manny squeezed through the crowd and emerged at the table. It looked for all the world to him as though they were in an embrace and a passionate kiss.

Horrified and speechless, Manny spun around, jostled his way out past the maître d's station, and stalked out the door. He was infuriated.

I should have stopped that travesty right then and there. And the potential liability to the firm. This cannot go unaddressed.

He got in his car out in the restaurant's parking lot and drove off, but after a few miles clicked on his Bluetooth and called Ella's cell phone number as he was descending from the crest of Mulholland Drive.

Five minutes later Ella Brooks was dead. And her own

cell phone smashed and incinerated in the burning hulk of her Porsche. It was ruled a fatal accident with the autopsy showing an elevated blood alcohol content in her corpse.

Another tragic, deadly DUI.

CHAPTER FIFTEEN

*The tragic class of LAIM probationary brokers
Suzie and Nancy huddle before their final
training session. The last week...*

B oth Nancy and Suzie had come into the office shortly after 6:00 to get ready before the financial markets opened at 6:30 PST. They had overnight account activity reports to examine, a few "at the open" trading orders to deal with, overnight futures to check on, all of the usual tasks to get their investing business moving for that day and that week. As usual, Suzie had poured over the Asian and other overseas stock market reports and trend lines.

The delayed redistribution of poor Art's accounts and client relationships had also been done, and each of them had less than a handful of those client statements to scrutinize so that they could make contact with the investors and introduce themselves as the newly assigned account managers. Normally those reassignments occurred within a very few days to enable the beginning of those new broker-client relationships and hopefully keep the accounts in LAIM before the investors drifted off to other firms. In this case, however, a short inquiry was made concerning the colleague who had accompanied Art on his Rodeo Drive shopping venture, to find out if there was any context to be concerned about regarding his unfortunate accident. Not that police had the slightest suggestion of any foul play.

By the time Art's client book had been scavenged and choicer relationships handed off to more senior brokers, there was not a large asset value passed on to Suzie and Nancy. Neither would be propelled past the finish line by what they got from Art's book. On the other hand, *anything* gave a positive nudge in the right direction. If nothing else, making up for the most recent market declines.

But by 8:45 they had each wrapped up the busyness of the start of the trading day, and they met privately in the ladies' room before going into the conference room where their training sessions were always held.

"Can you believe it? Can you believe it?" Suzie unleashed some of her pent-up distress and depressed feelings. "Now Ella's accidental death. I feel like the ancestors have cursed our poor group."

"I know," Nancy said. "I feel the same way. One of the firm's partners commented to me that they had never had a death occur in any year's probationary group, yet alone two horrible, accidental deaths. And then there was Jack's sad overdose. At least you and I are still standing."

"Yah, well, about that," Suzie maintained her down, depressed countenance. "I want you to be the first to know that I'm going to announce to Manny this morning in our session that I will be resigning and leaving the firm."

"No," Nancy gasped. "Why? What happened? You're the one best positioned to make it."

"Well, I can't do it immediately, I need the next few weeks, maybe up to a month, to conclude my client relationships in the most positive way. Help them with a transition. And I also have to wrap up other aspects of my current life here in the LA area. Bottom line, my dad is terminal with liver cancer, and there'll be some major adjustments for my mom, who is a stay-at-home wife. We probably have to put their Cerritos home up for sale and move her into a senior living facility. In any case, there'll be a lot for me to take care of, to take care of her, and no way I can continue with this round-the-clock, demanding, highly competitive line of work.

"But what about a leave of absence?" Nancy asked. "I think I, and others, could act as custodians of your relationships, keep things maintained until you work out the transitions. You've worked too hard and put so much of yourself into this to walk away so close to making it."

"I appreciate the suggestion and your kind encouragement," Suzie said. "But I would still be pulled back constantly. Worrying like I do about what's going on in the markets, checking on key stock positions, fussing about some of those clients who need a lot of handholding, on and on. I'm frankly depressed enough as it is, always having to keep the wolf of my own feelings outside the door.

"Besides, I actually have another job offer. In fact, at the facility my mom would move into. They need an office Business Manager, right up my alley with all of those administrative details. And I'd be there every day to support and help Mother. No. This is for the best. Trust me."

The two went into the conference room, and right after them Manny came in to do their final wrap-up training session. Rather than some detailed side issues of the investing/brokerage business, it was more of a summary, a "cleaning up" last meeting.

Plus, there were all of the other critical matters to deal with...including much to his surprise, the future resignation of his leading probationary broker. And Suzie had even scrounged up her last two necessary Financial Plans.

CHAPTER SIXTEEN

Last One Standing
Wednesday in the Los Angeles Investment
Management office,
the last week of probation...

Nancy Nighthawk sat quietly at her cubicle in the LAIM office near the Financial District in downtown Los Angeles. She had taken care of all of the urgent tasks, the early morning orders and trades, the overnight reports and updates, everything that needed doing ASAP that Wednesday. She caught her breath for a moment before turning to phone calls, emails, text messages, and a mutual fund field rep's video meeting to pitch their latest technological index fund.

Wow. First Jack's hospitalization and overdose. Then Art gets hit by a bus. Then Ella dies in that horrific accident up on Mulholland Drive. And now Suzie submits her notice and goes to take care of the mom, deal with her dad's death and estate, and take a new job. I feel like that James Fenimore Cooper's "Last of the Mohicans." But for how long? Friday I have to have all of the benchmarks met. And I'm still a few hundred thousand short on total book value of my accounts, plus not quite enough revenue brought in for both the firm and me. Suzie's accounts won't be reassigned until she actually leaves, so that wouldn't help me.

I guess the rest of my to-do list for today should include what I need to pack up of personal items in the next couple of days, get my account records ready to pass on to others, ah, let's see...

Her desk phone rang. "Nancy Nighthawk speaking..."

"Nancy Nighthawk of the Four Corners Navajo Nation?"

"Ah, well, Nancy Nighthawk of Los Angeles Investment Management, but yes, I'm originally from Navajoland in the Four Corners region. Who is this, please?"

"I'm Jonathan Billy. I'm the Chief Financial Officer for the Navajo Churro Sheepherders Cooperative. Are you able to set up an account for us at your brokerage firm? We have, oh, close to $900,000 sitting in a low-interest bank account in the Arizona Four Corners Monument Bank that we'd like to get a better return on.

"The placement of the money should be safe and conservative. It's a reserve fund from most of the many members of the cooperative and isn't drawn upon very often except for special needs. Maybe a few thousand or so a couple of times a year for special events and projects. But it's there in part to respond to possible emergencies among members, to finance annual fairs, things like that, so can't be exposed to any reckless risk."

Nancy tried to pick her jaw up off of her desktop. "Ah, well sure. I can help you with that. And I can make it economical, relatively low-cost for account maintenance, a small fee for my services. May I ask some questions and get some needed information from you?"

"Of course," Mr. Billy said. "Whatever you need."

"First of all, how did you get my name and number?"

"From your uncle, Jimmy Many Horses. Plus, several of

64

your relatives belong to us, and everybody vouches for your trustworthiness and hard work. And you may be an *Angeleno* now, but they all think of you as Navajolands."

Nancy took down all of the information needed for new account opening, including approximate amount to be wired in to LAIM, verifiable source of the money, investment policy statement adopted by the cooperative, signees for the account, their signatures authorizing the transfer and their authority to do transactions with the new account. Everything in place, faxed documents back and forth yet today, originals sent overnight by express mail, and the wire transfer could be done by Thursday, snugly placed in the new account and all ready to proceed by Friday. An initial sum could be available for immediate transactions that very day, the rest on temporary hold until compliance verified the entire balance as legit. Nancy would be the sole agent responsible for transactions on LAIM's end, with signed authorization on the part of the cooperative CFO for her to act on their behalf.

Remarkable, Nancy thought once the call was ended, and everything agreed upon. *And who says there aren't spirits of the ancestors at work in our lives yet today?* In her mind's eye she could picture herself on a pinto pony, on top of a Four Corners Navajoland mesa, looking out over red-rock desert, washed in bright sun, sky so blue that it put their local turquoise to shame, spirit-winds rustling the dry tumbleweed and bunch grass, puffs of white clouds rolling by in the distance. It was beautiful, awe-inspiring, humbling, and well, miraculous.

Almost as miraculous as the fact that, against all apparent odds, including her own struggles with anxiety disorder...Nancy Nighthawk was the last one standing.

CHAPTER SEVENTEEN

Manuel Taylor sums it all up
That same Wednesday afternoon...

Nancy had notified Manny of her remarkable, incredibly timely news before lunch on that Wednesday. And right after, the wire room to expect a sizable transfer of funds in the very near future. All of the new, necessary paperwork was in place by the end of the day. Things would settle very quickly, and she would literally be good to go...well, better yet, stay where she was. Except for moving into a new, private office along the outer wall, looking out at the downtown LA tall buildings on the outside, and in the opposite direction, the center cubicles, now noticeably emptier with the recent departure of the other members of her group.

Manny had the quiet that always descends rapidly on the office, as the trading day ends and the afternoon winds down, to reflect silently and privately on all that had happened with his five-member group of new, probationary brokers.

I almost blew it right from the start by telling Jack Johnson that he would feel better, get better faster, if he upped his dosage of that schizophrenia medicine. That he didn't have to get his psychiatrist's advice first, that they wouldn't allow him to have so many of the pills if they weren't perfectly safe to take. And that if one at a time was helping him to cope and function, even keep his job with us, that two at a time would surely get it done faster and better.

I only wanted him to experience a little set-back, slow his recovery down a little. Never meant for him almost to kick the bucket. Certainly, didn't set out to try to murder him. Oh, well, at least he's on the road to recovery now. And he wasn't going to make it in this business, anyway. Nice fellow. I'll send him another floral arrangement and "Best Wishes" card.

Manny counted on Jack being too embarrassed and too ashamed to tell anyone about Manny's pushing him on his medication. Plus, with the paranoia involved with his schizophrenia, anyone else would assume that he was remembering hallucinations, not reality.

I certainly had no way of knowing that Art would panic the way that he did at that jewelry store. I thought he would merely be detained for suspicion regarding that fancy Rolex. Maybe lose a couple of days or so of work here at LAIM, slow him down, too. All I needed was to have them get to the point that their accounts and client relationships would be reassigned sooner rather than later.

How was I to guess that Art would over-react, run out into the curbside bus stop, and get run over by an incoming bus? Damn, that was tough to see. Well, okay, tougher on him, I admit. Oh, yah, that's another note I should send, to his family, that we here at LAIM are thinking of him...and them in their grief.

And Ella. Well, Ella was too glitzy and too much of a

"looker" for her own good. All style, little substance. Having an "in" with the upper-crust crowd. Yah, but that doesn't carry over so well to their money. Those folks always want conservative, dependable, even boring, custodianship of their wealth. Once you have it, you don't want it going to those who simply don't have it...or even need it. Let them bootstrap their own way to money.

Speaking of "boring," that flashy bimbo thought I couldn't hear when she dissed my training sessions week-after-week. Thought they were "so boring-g." Well, her end wasn't so boring now, was it? Not that I knew that when I told her to drop dead, she would find such a spectacular way to do it for real.

Okay, when she told me that she had secured a meeting with Jay Armstrong that Friday evening up at Kramer's Skyline Supper Club, I knew who he was. I've been around the whole LA-Hollywood scene for decades, after all. It was worth a shot to see if she actually did have an in, a line, on landing some of his investment accounts. Besides, it's always a nice place to go.

And I also knew of his reputation and taste for much younger women, actresses, models, wannabe's, sometimes one on each arm. Didn't know if he would so blatantly make a play for her, but I would have put some of my cash reserve on it. Didn't surprise me. What I don't know, I admit, is whether she succumbed to it and that hot kiss was consensual, or harassment by a well-known sexual predator. Well, didn't matter. Gave me the excuse I needed to fire her on the spot. Oh, "fire." Maybe unfortunate choice of words. But such destruction of her cell phone should have eliminated any trace and possible suspicion that I was involved in any way in her fatal accident. All I really wanted was her gone. And she is.

Now I could have lived and accomplished what I

needed with the three of them out of the picture. Plus, I figured that Nancy would hang in there until this Friday and then have to be washed out. Natural attrition. But what a turnaround. Suzie turns in her notice when I assumed she would be the one to cross the finish line successfully, and at the last-minute Nancy pulls her young career out of the trash fire with a miraculous, need I say, surprise gift, a substantial account. Manny shook his head, smiled, and shrugged. *You just don't always know what cards will end up being played in this game.*

What he needed to orchestrate and accomplish if possible was, frankly, to boost his monthly cash income. His own acquisition of any new clients and new accounts was a rare event due to his many other responsibilities at LAIM. Assistant Branch Manager administrative duties. The weekly training classes for new, probationary brokers. Coordination of the brokerage team in general. Special tasks delegated to him by the Branch Manager or some other of the McIntosh family members. Once in a great while one would land in his lap by a word-of-mouth referral from one of his own long-time clients, but only once in a while.

So, a possible route to pick up such a boost as he sorely needed was to have younger, lower-tenure brokers and portfolio managers be "washed out," fail to meet firm standards and requirements, resign for whatever reason...or tragically, regrettably, suffer some career-ending catastrophe. Didn't have to be death, but that could work.

Then Manny could be in a position to siphon off an early portion of their accounts and investment assets to be reassigned to him. Not too many so as to appear inappropriate, suspicious, or downright greedy to the partners. But he could occasionally "cherry pick" some choice relationships that would be real cash generators for their broker, like especially good broker "trails" that paid a portion of the fund fee to him each month. Or someone with a hefty cash supply who would be a good target for selling them an annuity with a life insurance company. Those paid good cash bonuses upfront to the salesperson, plus a trailing sum on a regular basis.

As he had been upfront about telling the probationary group, it was historically true that only two, or at most three, and sometimes only one, would be the last to stand successful at the end. This group was especially fortuitous for him, particularly when nudged, maneuvered, okay, manipulated in the right, disastrous directions. His own client book of income-generating accounts had just about "burped" with the reassignments he had so recently benefited from.

And it was all so invisible, unsuspected by anyone else, including the "victims." No one seemed to realize that Manuel Taylor could be professionally categorized as a "social predator," a social manipulator who was undiagnosed with antisocial personality disorder.

He almost got away with it.

A week later, he stood at his office door and stared down toward Nancy in her new window office. He watched two detective investigators walking straight in his direction.

It was one of those "perfect storm" kind of convergences of unlikely, separated events. An attendant at the psychiatric unit of the Cedars Sinai clinic remembered overhearing some low conversation between Jack Johnson and another man about self-medicating. Another look at Art Tarrington's fatal encounter with the Metro bus had suggested a follow up interview with Manny about the circumstances that pushed Art toward the "accident." And Ella's cell phone had been smashed and scorched in that terrible accident, but the chip or memory card that stored gigabytes of her calls was still retrievable. So not destroyed was evidence of her last call with Manny.

Did any of these things point toward an indictable crime? Hours of interrogation and dot-connecting would tell.

Even in a new, electronic, high-tech world, chickens still come home to roost.

The End

EPILOGUE

Like my previous novellas - *Cellaring, Death in the Dinner Group, Swarm*, this novella was planned to be a combined genre of murder/death mystery story and a consideration of the tremendously overlooked and neglected pandemic of mental disorders, mental disability, and mental health issues in general. As I have stated previously, it is a global, national, regional, municipal, family, tribal, clan and personal crisis that touches virtually 100% of human beings, either directly, or closely through others.

If by chance, dear reader, you had the opportunity to read one of those earlier novellas and their Epilogues, you might remember such facts and statistics as scientific researcher estimates that approximately one billion of the world's population is directly affected by these mental disorders and issues. It is even bigger and more severe than the coronavirus pandemic that still rages as these words are written. I will not repeat here all of those statistical details.

The fact of the matter, however, is that this mental disorder crisis extends its impact in a huge number of ways that, again, are far too often unrecognized, glossed over, and lost in other, more attention-getting details. For only one example among a tremendous number of phenomena, another social, racial, political, extremely personal plague that is so egregious and outrageous going on today is gun violence. For centuries past, and certainly terrorizing us into the foreseeable future, it is a horrific fixture in American society. And especially in African American and other communities of color.

A recent *Washington Post* comprehensive study and subsequent article points out that beginning in the well-researched period of 2015-present, the number of American people shot and killed by police shootings has continued at amazingly the same number across the country each of those years. Despite large-scale, widespread community and police department efforts and expenditures directed toward such things as "de-escalation" training, changeovers in big-city police leadership, a nationwide push for criminal justice reform, police use reform, efforts to curb police brutality, use of force standards, and re-training again, the numbers of people fatally shot by police has continued stubbornly at the level of 1000-1100 each year.

The reason for mentioning that national tragedy and too-often injustice here is the number of those victims killed by police while in mental distress. About one in four, over 25%, had some identifiable mental health issue/disorder, far in excess of the percentage of citizens in general afflicted with mental disorders. Truth is, if a person suffers from mental disorder - traditionally referred to as "illness" - they are more likely to be shot and possibly killed by law enforcement. And that is only one of the terrible consequences of mental health issues.

Each of the characters depicted in this novella, *Last One Standing,* was written to suggest that they possessed one of the five most common mental illnesses. Only one of them in the storyline was described as receiving mental health care and treatment by mental health professionals. That fictional detail was deliberate to illustrate that the considerable majority of mental disorders among people in the United States, and even more, around the world, go undiagnosed, untreated, and unaddressed or even recognized. And the number of individuals experiencing mental illness around the globe continues to grow.

By now, an estimated 300 million people on Planet Earth and 3 million in the US are impacted by **depression,** the most common mental disorder. In this story, the character Susan Whitsun was depicted as being affected by some degree of depression or depressive disorder and severe stress disorder. She was described as living and dealing with depressed or "low" moods, worry, heightened concern about her future, feeling discouraged and "down" out of proportion to her actual situation.

As is the case with the other characters as written, this author is not qualified, nor presumes any authority, to make clinically precise definitions and descriptions of depressive disorder or stress disorder in the character of Suzie. And it has to be emphasized that all people have "ups" and "downs" in their lives at different points. Just because someone feels rather depressed or discouraged sometimes does not necessarily mean that they would be diagnosed professionally as having a depressive disorder. But if exhibited more frequently and more severely than might be typical for mentally healthy persons, negatively impacting their ability to function in their lives and work...it's possible they do.

The second most common mental disorder is **anxiety**, affecting 40 million adults every year in America alone. Anxiety disorders are said to be diagnosed and treated for scarcely more than a third of those who are forced to live with them. And that is tragic for a number of reasons, including that they are highly treatable with psychotherapy and medication.

Nancy Nighthawk was written to suggest an issue with anxiety disorder. While "fear" is generally a reaction to a specific, observable danger or threat, "anxiety" doesn't need a "triggering" stimulus. In fact, it is often experienced about things that will never actually affect the person. It is driven by feelings of "what if..." or "the unknown." Nancy worried constantly about what might happen, what could happen, regarding all kinds of things. It was a generalized anxiety disorder.

Arthur Tarrington was depicted as displaying at least the beginning stages of the third most common mental disorder, **bipolar affective disorder**. Bipolar people present both manic, "up," episodes and depressive ones. And while the mood swings can switch from one to the other quickly, sometimes there are intervals of "normal" or stabilized moods in between. It is a disorder that affects approximately 60 million people worldwide.

As you read, Art could experience a time of mania when he felt elevated about himself, his self-esteem, and his work. He could be hyperactive, feeling less need for sleep or "breaks," and be prone to making poor decisions like shopping sprees or unwise purchases. When in a depressive episode, he felt "down," with less energy, frankly, having trouble sleeping. He could be discouraged to the point of desperation.

As expressed in the storyline, it is also "normal" for everyone to have ups and downs in life and work. Everyone has moods, admittedly some more pitched in one direction or the other. Everyone experiences times of feeling both encouraged and discouraged. Only a minority of persons are diagnosable - if they are ever examined and diagnosed by a mental health professional like a psychiatrist - as bipolar, but they are a minority numbering in those many millions.

Jack Johnson was the one character in the story diagnosed and initially treated for his mental disorder, although he was manipulated into suffering a medication overdose. He had joined about 23 million other people around the world impacted by psychoses, specifically **schizophrenia**. And as was typical for those folks, Jack's thinking was distorted by hallucination, delusion, and paranoia that impaired his daily functioning. He could hear "voices" within his head, convinced that they came from unknown, invisible persons. A person like Jack would require lifelong treatment...but only a small minority of sufferers actually receive that needed care.

Schizophrenia is an extremely serious mental disorder that makes people interpret reality abnormally and be greatly compromised in their ability to distinguish between reality and fantasy, a sense of mental "fragmentation." And the fantasy can seem like the "real" reality. It is far too common in the United States alone, and can't be cured, only treated as a chronic condition. Many, perhaps even most, do not even realize that they are unwell. Consequently, it can be hard to convince the sufferer to take their medication consistently. They may even fear that it is intended to harm, not help.

The risk of suffering schizophrenia rises if one of a person's parents also suffers from it. And it is much more prevalent among homeless persons. There is no way, obviously, of knowing with certainty, but it is estimated to affect perhaps twenty percent of the homeless, which means thousands of people in America living homeless and with schizophrenia every day.

And finally, the fifth most common mental disorder is **dementia**. It is another chronic, progressive mental disorder that involves deterioration of cognitive functioning beyond what normally happens in aging. Dementia is estimated to impact 50 million people globally, 3 million cases in the US. The decline in memory, orientation, comprehension, calculation, and language is inevitably accompanied by a deterioration of emotional and social control. No cure is available for this disorder either, but treatment and care can ease the suffering and the confusion.

No one among the characters of this story was described as having dementia, although some of Manuel Taylor's thinking and behavior could suggest the beginning of dementia. Particularly his inappropriate, negative behavior, callousness, and even manipulation and uncaring about the results he was inflicting upon others. He *was* referred to as being undiagnosed but affected by **antisocial personality disorder**.

ASPD, as it's known, is also common, involving more than 200,000 cases per year in America. And it is yet another disorder that can't be cured, requires a medical diagnosis, however unlikely to occur, and can last for years or be lifelong. Those with ASPD are prone to break laws, act impulsively, and lack consideration for the safety or fate of others. Simply put, such people have blatant disregard for norms of right and wrong, exploit others, and manipulate for personal gain or even pleasure.

Finally, and again, all-too-common mental disorders - what I insist upon calling a largely hidden and overlooked worldwide pandemic - are simply everywhere and affecting/impacting everyone. Whether you and I recognize it or not. And unlike other illnesses like coronaviruses, mental disorders are universally accompanied by stigma, discrimination, social exclusion, shaming, denial, and tremendously insufficient resources to alleviate and cure what could possibly be cured.

We all ignore, minimize, and neglect this mental health pandemic to our own peril and diminishment. And its tentacles of human pain, suffering and devastation extend around and within all of us. Meaningful, helpful, healing action is paramount.

Murder
and
Big Momma

Chapter One

A soft dusk had settled on Wigwam Lake and the northern forest surrounding it. The setting sun had slipped below the horizon of distant dark pines and mixed hardwoods, leaving a fading pink glow in the southwestern sky. The first bright stars flickered above in the black sky, but the crescent moon had not yet risen. A faint breeze stirred ripples across the surface of the shadowy water, adding to the widening wake of his fourteen-foot, vintage wooden boat as Kenny rowed slowly along the underwater crest of the rocky bar ten feet below.

She should be down there somewhere, he thought hopefully. *Come on, Big Momma. Fat, juicy, wobbling suckers. Just waiting for your toothy jaws to open up and bite down.*

He was referring to the footlong wooden lures that trailed at the end of wire leaders and stout monofilament lines that stretched back from nine-foot graphite rods that extended on either side of his rowboat. The lures were hand-carved, painted to resemble lake suckers. They were a favorite prey of the big muskellunge and northern pike that occupied the fertile lakes that are heavily scattered throughout the Northern Wisconsin forest. Three strong, sharp, treble hooks dangled beneath each of the lures he was trolling. He kept the hooks honed sharp enough to dig into the boney hard jaws of the big fish when they struck. That is, if they went for a mouthful of delicious prey for their meal.

He would lean forward in the middle seat of the boat. Slip his oars simultaneously, smoothly, almost silently, into the surface of the water. Take a slow, steady pull. Lean back. Lift the oars at the end of the stroke. Lean forward again, lifting the dripping oars quietly out of the water. He would then wait until the boat glided forward in its path and slowed almost to a stop, pushing that wake outward in a V-shape.

The trolled lures, meanwhile, were hand-set with their small, metal "tails" so that one would dive down a foot or so below the surface of the water with each stroke of the oars. Then it would wobble forward in the direction that the boat was going, before rising up toward the surface in a slow wobble until it reached, or almost reached, the top. It mimicked a wounded sucker, a bait fish trying to swim down toward the bottom of the lake, but too injured to make it. It would flail weakly back up to the surface. The second lure on the other side of the boat's wake was set so that it would "swim" a couple of feet deeper in the water. It produced the same "action" as an injured meal, wobbling and weakly trying to swim through the water.

In each case, the hope on the part of the trolling angler was that both of the lures would resemble an easy meal to a large, top-of-the-line predator fish like the giant Northern Muskellunge that Kenny targeted so fervently. "Muskies" are the ultimate trophy fish in that North Woods country.

As "apex predators" in the waters in which they live, they are comparatively rare. Even the best musky lakes with the most favorable habitat and prey for them will support at most one musky per acre of surface water. Because of their rarity, the Wisconsin Department of Natural Resources placed a catch limit of one Musky of at least forty inches a day per angler. At that large size the musky will likely have reached an impressive weight of more than fifteen pounds.

Their relative scarcity, high-set size limits to be legally taken, and an innate, natural tendency to be "moody" or hard to tempt to a lure, have made the fish exceedingly difficult to harvest. The musky is legendarily the "fish of a thousand casts," but innumerable anglers over many years will testify that that number is set way too low. Thousands and thousands of casts, over years and years of earnestly trying, may still not result in an angler being able to catch a "legal" musky.

In the words of many summer cabin and cottage owners, "I've been coming up here my entire life, and I've never been able to catch a legal musky."

Another goal fueled Ken's obsession. This evening, he was fishing on Wigwam Lake, one of several lakes where the minimum size limit was even higher - 50 inches for a musky to be a "keeper." But even that size, causing the toothy fish to weigh perhaps 35-40 pounds and be considered "gargantuan," was below his sights.

Kenny was after "Big Momma."

Big Momma had only been sighted a few times by anglers and boaters on Wigwam Lake, a gorgeous, fertile lake of about 700 acres. But her reputation had spread throughout the bars, bait and tackle shops, fishing clubs, resorts, and marinas scattered across the northern reaches of the state. Professional fishing guides and the most dedicated anglers who like to consider themselves "musky addicts" talked often about the legendary fish. Some of them didn't like the "buzz," because they didn't want the attention and increased fishing pressure on Wigwam trying to get her.

And frankly, many of them felt that if she was going to be caught, they should be the one to do it.

Like the eternal, proverbial "fishing story," Big Momma had a fantastic tendency to grow in size in much of the buzz about her. Some, perhaps encouraged and fueled by their favorite alcohol and traditional anglers' hyperbole, claimed that she had to be a new world's record. Many, including a few who had actually spotted her in the lake when she rarely swam up to the surface, estimated that she would easily top fifty pounds. The truth was that if she was ever able to be measured and weighed, she would register 54-55 inches and perhaps a pound or two over that fifty-pound estimate.

Across the entire state of Wisconsin, "capital" of musky fishing, there were years when absolutely no one caught the elusive to the extreme "fifty-pounder."

Kenny had spent a few decades pursuing trophy muskies. He had caught a few "thirty pounders" and one that went almost forty. If he could somehow put Big Momma into his boat and onto a registered scale at his favorite tackle shop, it would be the achievement of a lifetime.

And, although he didn't care nearly as much about this part, it would also be tremendously profitable and "enshrine" him as a musky fishing celebrity. There would be awards, magazine articles and photos. He could be invited to appear on television fishing shows, or at least the regional broadcast news. He might be invited to endorse lure and fishing tackle and be featured in advertising. There was also the possibility of a book. He would get celebrity attention at spring fishing shows, with autographs and "selfies" galore.

Kenny already enjoyed a limited reputation among fervent anglers and long-time musky hunters, but Big Momma would inevitably propel him to fame. It didn't hurt that a national fishing hall of fame presented a prize to the "lucky" angler who registered a bona fide fifty-pounder. It paid one hundred dollars per pound if they could put the mounted fish in their museum and feature it and its captor (all expenses paid) at fishing conventions.

But Kenny wasn't thinking about all of that as he row-trolled over the sunken bar with its lush clumps of aquatic cabbage weed growing up from the stony bottom. Cabbage weed provides a food chain buffet. A variety of aquatic insect larvae thrived among its leaves. Crawdads and water bugs ate the insect larvae. Minnows and small panfish, fed on the insects and crustaceans. Predatory fish like walleyes, northerns, and muskies came especially for the minnows and panfish. Muskies favored the soft-bodied and slower-moving sucker fish that dwell and feed on weedy bars.

Kenny hoped that Big Momma would be visiting the bar and its diverse buffet this evening, coming up from the depths under the cover of the darkening night. Although the dark of night was not really the favorite time for a majority of anglers to be on the water, he had often hooked into a good musky in the evening. So, he didn't mind extending his fishing time, despite the fact that he had already been rowing and trolling for several hours on Wigwam.

As he reached the far end of the underwater bar, which he could see on the dim light of his depth and fish finding gauge, he also spotted a comparatively large blip that appeared several yards behind the boat, at a level a bit below where his shallow lure was set to dive and wobble and rise and dive. He strained to see something, any different disturbance in the wake of the boat.

There. Is that a bulge in the water? Behind the lure? Near where it surfaced?

He focused, ready to take the rod on that side out of its angled holder if a strike occurred. Ready to grab, set the hook, and have the stout rod bend over sharply in the fight of a lifetime. It was as intense of a focus as Kenny had ever been capable of. Absolute, complete concentration and attention.

This could be it!

Crash!

Kenny Cranston never heard the other boat approach from his starboard, open lake side until it was already upon him. The boat hit his rowboat mid-gunnel, crunching through the antique wood strips. Kenny was propelled into the water on the port side. The other boat continued over the capsized rowboat, striking Kenny with a fatal blow to his skull. His body was sent floating, drifting, and gradually sinking among the cabbage weeds.

The murderous pilot of the offensive boat circled once in the dark, shining a flashlight across the debris. Assured of Kenny's death, they took off for a distant landing, leaving the scene and the sinking rowboat.

Eerie quiet, the rippled water, and scattered debris from the collision were all that remained near the underwater bar.

Big Momma had left quickly and silently unseen by anyone.

Chapter Two

The Guides' Table and John Jenkins

It was unofficial, no signs or verbal statements from bartenders or bouncers, but "The Fishing Hole" bar had a pecking order and table segmentation. The long, brass-railed, vintage bar itself was open territory. Sit where you want, although a few "regulars" had their favorite stools. Most of the scattered tables, especially toward the main door and near the swinging doors in and out of the kitchen, were also "first come, first serve." A couple of back tables against the varnished log walls with their patina of age were understood by year-round residents and long-time summer people and vacationers as "reserved," unofficially, for local shop and resort owners, town officials, and a few distinguished guests.

Large mounted-fish and photos of successful anglers adorned the log walls bordering a table tucked in the back corner. For decades, a fifty-pound mounted muskie hung near the darkened antique tin ceiling, high above this table and far away from the busiest hustle and bustle of the bar.

It was the Guides' Table.

Seldom did anyone else but seasoned, honored, professional fishing guides ever sit at that table. And if someone ignorantly did so, well, there was no official, stated policy that they couldn't. But more than one had wondered why such an otherwise friendly, welcoming establishment would have glares and expressions of disapproval turned in their direction.

The night after the murder of Kenneth Cranston out on Wigwam Lake, John "Johnny" Jenkins, Andy Nash, and Sven Karlsson took their accustomed places at the Guides Table. Bob, the long-time server at The Fishing Hole, soon showed up with their habitual choices - brandy for both Johnny and Andy, Swedish vodka for Sven. As they each took an initial sip and savored the potent drinks, Christine O'Malley showed up and grabbed the remaining chair at the round table.

Chris was virtually a token woman in the unofficial fraternity, not that she would ever stand for even a hint of being regarded as "token." In one of seemingly countless male-dominated endeavors, a woman fishing guide was possibly one of the rarest. But she had wiggled her way into the group, at least "on the fringes," over time because she loved to fish, and she had both passion and skill.

Clients found her hardworking and personable. Male anglers found her both able and attractive. Andy wanted to date her. Johnny didn't really approve. There had never been a female fishing guide in the North Woods in his earlier decades. But she had worn down his resistance by seeming like a daughter, flattering him for advice, and at least sometimes buying his brandy. The last part had probably been the clincher.

Johnny was the patriarch of the group. In his late-seventies, he had been a professional fishing guide for going-on half a century in Boulder Crossing, one of the primary claimants of the title, "Musky Capital of the World," in Northern Wisconsin. Johnny had been guiding "sports" for so long and had spent countless days out on the waters of area lakes, that his skin was permanently dark, leathery, and deeply wrinkled. He was a wiry man, once five-foot-seven, in the peak of his youth, but now shrunken to only about five-five. His deep-set dark brown eyes crowned with thick, bushy, grey eyebrows, could twinkle with subtle humor and gnome-like mischievousness. Or they could glare black fury, if he felt disrespected, cheated, patronized, or otherwise treated like the old man he really was.

One thing that had really gotten under his skin in recent years was bar altercations. His ancestry was Cornish. And like the famous Cornish or banty roosters, he had always possessed an aggressive streak out of proportion to his small size. This especially happened when he had more of his favorite brandy than he should. His hackles would rise if any bar patron so much as suggested that he was too old for anything. What made it worse and drove him to distraction, was that literally everyone, whether natives or summer people, thought it nuts to get into a fight with a little man well into his seventies.

"No one will do me the respect of even giving me a shove," he once complained to companions at the Guides Table. And that frustration tended to fuel his natural aggressiveness.

Predictably perhaps, he had a strong preference for old, traditional things, especially in his guide work. For decades he had operated out of an antique, Adirondack-style, wooden plank strip guide boat. He had upgraded it over the years with a modern, four-stroke, 30 horsepower Mercury outboard motor and top line trolling motor. But he still liked to use the long, antique wooden oars for easing quietly along shorelines with the sudden drop-offs that muskies so often cruised for meals.

He would gruffly but expertly direct his sports – only one or two in his boat at a time. Where to cast. How to work their lures. How to respond if a musky followed a lure being retrieved. How to fight the fish if it struck and was hooked. How to bring the fish, when it tired, up to range of his big landing net. And he grumbled audibly when the poor, inexperienced angler usually bungled some part of the whole process, including when to stand and when to sit in his boat.

Despite the fact that he had passed his prime and his most noteworthy successes occurred a considerable number of years ago, Johnny treasured his hard-earned reputation as a "classic" fishing guide. Two of the old photos on the wall behind the Guides Table featured Johnny with unknown anglers alongside of a large musky hanging from a horizontal pole, held up by grinning anglers celebrating the rare capture of such a magnificent trophy.

But they were from years and years ago. Oh, he still took sports out, and every once in a while, his party would bring a legal musky into one of the local bait and tackle shops for measuring, weighing on a registered scale, and proud display in the shop's glass-topped freezer or refrigerated display case. But on those rare occasions the fish would always be *jusst* legal size, maybe an inch or a fraction more.

Even in his "glory" days, Johnny himself or one of his sports had never caught the holy grail of a fifty pounder. Forty-five pounds was his absolute best, and only one of those, twenty-some years ago. Guiding someone to a fifty pounder would be the ultimate accomplishment of his long career. Time was running out for that unlikely event to occur.

He had heard a wild rumor of a gargantuan musky in the lake but chalked it up to being the all-too-common "fish story."

"There's never been a fifty-pounder caught on Wigwam in all my years," he had said one evening at the Guides Table. "If there's such a fish anywhere in the state these days, it would be on the flowage, or maybe the Eagle River chain. Not Wigwam," he scoffed.

Then one day, on Wigwam Lake with a rich lawyer from Chicago, Johnny caught a glimpse of Big Momma. Late in the afternoon of that day, there she was, suspiciously scrutinizing his sport's jerk bait

Gauging whether it was really an injured, laboring yellow perch...or an imposter, like the lure that had almost snagged her when Big Momma was a younger, smaller, version of herself. She followed curiously, tentatively, not yet ready to flip her internal switch that would result in a savage lunge for the bait. Then easing back, slowing, and finally finning down deeper into the depths and disappearing. It was as if the "off" switch had been clicked shut.

Phony was somehow her verdict. She was gone.

The rich client's heart sank with a disappointment that actually surpassed the day that he had lost a multi-million-dollar verdict in a civil court judgment. At least on that occasion he had still collected a fat fee for all of his billable hours. But that giant musky would have been his fish of a lifetime. Bragging rights until the day he died. Probably worthy of mention at his memorial service...if any member of his family had the sense to lift up what was really important in his life.

Johnny had merely said at the time, "Tough luck. They do that. More times than not."

But the precise spot of the lake had burned indelibly into his memory. Muskies tend to be very territorial. Like all kinds of predators, the biggest fish preferred the prime feeding spots and often chased lesser fish away. He would come back, looking for Big Momma on that rocky, cabbage weed-covered bar, whenever he could.

And on an evening off, that all-too-rare occasion, this is where I'll be. Even better if I can catch it myself. This will be my trophy, one way or another.

The reality, of course, was that there was no way Johnny or anyone else could put up a "Reserved" sign on that underwater bar on Wigwam Lake. Nor a fin tag on Big Momma saying, "Johnny Jenkins' trophy one day, hands off!"

Anyone might fish there - guide, client, veteran musky hunter, or some young kid messing around on vacation his first day on the lake. And, if they somehow caught the giant fish, well the fishing gods are fickle and favor not necessarily the bold, but whomever they randomly choose.

Still, Johnny didn't shrink one little bit from telling his colleagues and fellow musky hunters that he considered Big Momma to be *his* to go after. He couldn't keep anyone else from trying to catch her, but they could at least know that he wouldn't like it in the least if they succeeded.

And he knew how to keep a white-hot grudge.

Chapter Three

Andy Nash, the "Paul Bunyan" of musky guides

Andy Nash was practically the polar opposite of John Jenkins in more ways than one. He was a giant of a man. A former college football lineman, until he blew out his knee in a game, he stood six-foot, five, with a barrel chest and big muscles...these days accompanied by the proverbial "beer belly." He wore his curly, red-brown hair long, often unkempt, along with a full beard. Year-round he preferred wide suspenders, checkered shirts, canvas cloth logger's style pants, and work boots. He cut a very Paul Bunyan-like figure, and it was something he grew to cultivate, including in his brochures and regional "attractions" circulars, as well as Chamber of Commerce materials.

He was something of a celebrity in the North Woods. Tourists mostly asked him to pose with them for photos. He was also featured in a number of regular community and area events, like Fourth of July parades, "Musky Days," fishing tournaments, and Colorama festivals in late September/early October in the little towns of the area.

Andy was relatively young, mid-thirties, and came from a moneyed family. His father was a successful developer and was not supportive of Andy's decision to be a professional fishing guide. As a conservative suit-and-tie country club member, he was not thrilled with Andy's "cartoonish" personal style. Andy's mom refused to let her only son be cut off. So, Andy was well-funded in his North Woods life and work. He loved to fish, to be a regional celebrity, and to sit at the Guides Table.

Particularly at supper time in the early evening when the exclusive gathering of guides would convene, it was not unusual for parents to bring their small children over and ask to take their little ones' picture with "Paul Bunyan." Johnny would always shake his head disgustedly, but Andy loved the attention. And paired with the fawning devotion of an over-indulgent mother since early childhood, frankly he assumed that he deserved it

Andy could afford to start from scratch as an independent fishing guide, strictly on his own. Even at the beginning, when no one really knew him and his client base struggled to rise from absolutely nothing to a few now and then, he didn't have to worry about "making it." He was hyper competitive, had always been so from his childhood days playing PeeWee football in the Chicago suburbs, and never agonized over whether he could be successful. Moreover, he had learned from that early age, and from a driving father, to practice hard, to work hard, to want it more than the other guy, and to never quit. He had competed his entire life for whatever he wanted. Football, girls, social status, fame, becoming established as a North Woods musky guide. Once he heard about the rare sightings of Big Momma in Wigwam Lake...well, he would make any effort, any effort whatsoever, to compete and win to capture her.

He had all of the tools, bells, and whistles to get the job done. With his mother's "anything you need, dear" attitude, early on in his guiding career, he had put out thousands of dollars to buy the best fishing boat for his needs, with motorized tilt bed trailer. To tow the boat and trailer, he acquired a brand-new Jeep Gladiator double-cab, go-anywhere truck. It would also transport as many as three sports and all the necessary gear and tackle.

No quaint, nostalgic, classic Adirondack wooden guide boat for him, Andy had purchased a top-of-the-line Skeeter Bass Boat. It had two casting platforms, pre-mounted electric trolling motor, and was driven by a F60 60hp Midrange Yamaha outboard motor, equipped with Variable Trolling RPM switch. He had the racy-looking boat customized with artist-designed hull lettering: *Andy's Musky Catcher*. The same lettering style was custom painted on the cab doors of his truck, with slight alteration: *Andy's Musky Transport*. Other guides and area business people thought his whole style flashy and over-the-top.

Johnny would shake his head, "Damn showman," but he tolerated the big kid.

When they were side-by-side at a landing, at the bait shop, or standing up at the Guides Table, Andy and Johnny were the very personification of a Mutt and Jeff duo - the giant flamboyant showman, and the diminutive banty rooster, balding, wizened curmudgeon. People, whether locals or vacationers, loved it.

Around twenty-four hours after the deliberate, fatal crashing of Kenneth Cranston's wooden rowboat, the conversation at the Guide's Table exclusively concerned Kenny's demise.

Andy brought it up, never shy about speaking in any situation. "You all heard about Kenny Cranston?"

"God, yes," gasped Christine, "the poor man. What a terrible accident. Do they know how it happened?"

"Investigation's still ongoing," Andy said. "But we've all seen him out in that old wooden rowboat of his. Probably didn't have any good running lights. Or hadn't gotten around to turning them on with night falling."

Andy's rig had enough lights and flags to qualify as a float for one of the area holiday parades. And more than once had been lined up in those parades.

Johnny harrumphed in his usual gruff manner, and true to his aggressive nature, countered with, "Brought it on himself. Damn fool."

Sven Karlsson was by nature the quietest member of the group, and despite his intellect was often hesitant to speak up. As usual, he was the best informed about all subjects that were raised at the table.

"The Wisconsin State Patrol, the County Sheriff's Water Safety Patrol, and the Department of Natural Resources Boat Enforcement Patrol are all present out there on Wigwam. A joint investigation. Alex, the township constable, was first on the scene with his patrol boat. He was called in last night by some recreational boaters when they spotted the debris floating on the surface in the fading light."

"Oh, we all know Alex," Andy hooted. "What a joke. Strutting around in his uniform and badge."

"Oh, he's not so bad," Christine said. "He tries to be conscientious about his duties."

"Too fond of passing out them damn tickets," Johnny grumbled.

Alex had ticketed all of the professional guides at least once for boating regulation violations. Some examples included motoring too fast in a "No Wake" zone with some clients who were in a hurry, or failure to have running or warning lights turned on as darkness fell in the evening. But most of Alex's targets in the performance of his water safety duties were careless or inebriated tourists or self-proclaimed "big shots" who liked to think that rules, even safety regs, were for the "little people."

Andy realized that Sven was usually better informed than most folks around the area, even if Sven wasn't confident about speaking up much of the time. Andy asked him if he knew more. "You hearing any cause for what happened?"

Christine interrupted, "And have they found the poor man's body?"

Sven flustered at their barrage.

"Ah, ah, well, yes, the coroner has his body, and there'll be an autopsy to confirm cause of death," he said. "And, ah, rumors or possibly leaks, ah, suggest that it was a tragic accident. Probably some tourist. Not watching where they were going. And too afraid to own up to hitting someone else's boat."

"Or someone not liking that Kenny was trying to go after Big Momma," Andy said in a phony sinister tone and a poke in Johnny's direction.

The jab wasn't lost on Johnny. "Wouldn't have happened if he wasn't trying that," he shot back.

"Well, it's too bad," Christine said. "Kenneth was well-known for a lot of years among veteran musky hunters, and he really worked hard for the fish he managed to put on the scales. All of those hours of row-trolling that old boat. Few put in that kind of physical effort and dedication to the sport."

"And look how he ended up," Johnny said cynically. "All those years and all of that work, and what did he gain from all of that?" The others weren't sure that Johnny was talking only about Ken Cranston at that point.

Andy couldn't help himself. "I agree with Johnny. Why all of that effort and sacrifice going after Big Momma? If anyone's going to put her in the display case at Wayne's Bait and Tackle, it's going to be me." He smiled and stuck his thumbs under his suspenders in a confident gesture.

Johnny glared at him, shook his head, but didn't offer a comeback. *Damn cocky son-of-a-bitch.* But it was hard even for a patriarch cherishing grandiose memories of past glory not to like Andy...at least some of the time. He was entertaining in an obnoxious, full-of-himself kind of way.

Chapter Four

Sven Karlsson, the dour Swede

Sven Karlsson was a fourth generation Swede in the Boulder Crossing area. His great-grandfather Ole had emigrated to Northern Wisconsin near the end of World War I along with several other native Swedes. They found the forest and lake country reminiscent of their ancestral lands around Stockholm, called the "Venice of the North" for its many lakes and waterways set in deciduous forest land with numerous pine trees as well. Like a good number of Swedes who were avid anglers, some commercially, Ole had captained a trawler fishing the now-declining cod stocks in the Baltic Sea. Sven always believed that he had fishing in his blood and the marrow of his Viking bones.

Despite the lore that Swedes were tall, blond, and athletic, Sven was average height, about five foot nine, muscular and active, but not greatly athletic. He did feature brownish-blond hair, however, and a personality that was reserved, quiet much of the time, studious, and too often insecure. He had a dry sense of humor, but since he was hesitant about expressing it, he fit the cliche of a dour Swede with a severe demeanor that some people mistook for being humorless. He couldn't help but worry at times about how he came across to others.

A resort owner on the nearby chain of lakes was of Finnish ancestry, other emigrants who had settled in the area since the late 1800's, and he felt a Scandinavian connection with Sven. So, a number of years ago the resort owner had hired him as a resort fishing guide. In that capacity, Sven's clients were mostly guests staying in the lodge or cabins of the resort. Since he had established a reputation of being a productive guide, others could request a spot in his schedule and did so fairly often. First priority went to resort guests, however.

The other regulars at the Guides Table possessed a slight tendency to regard Sven as not *quite* their equal, since he was not "making it on his own," but had "built-in" clientele. That unspoken prejudice, combined with his natural reserve and insecurity, contributed to Sven's tendency to settle into the background of the professional fishing guides' world. He couldn't help a nagging worry in the back of his mind and psyche that he didn't really belong with the likes of Johnny, Andy, or even the gregarious Christine. Sven envied the long-established status of Johnny Jenkins, and the flamboyant showmanship of Andy. While he was more attracted to than intimidated by Christine, he envied her too, for her outgoing personality, genuine flair, and ability to put fish in the live box for her clients. She made them feel good about their experience with her out on the area waters.

Quite in contrast to Johnny and his classic, antique Adirondack guide boat, and Andy with his flashy, state-of-the-art bass boat and rig, Sven's employment at the resort made it pretty much mandatory that he use one of the resort's fleet of deep-V Alumacraft fishing boats. The sixteen-footer assigned to him was adequately equipped with one of the resort's 4ohp Evinrude outboard motors, a serviceable trolling motor, and other necessary equipment like electronic fish finder, landing nets, gaff, live box, etc. But everyone knew it wasn't really *his* boat.

One thing Sven knew. If he or one of his clients staying at the resort could go on Wigwam and land Big Momma...if the Norse god of sea and fishing, Njord, would bless this descendant of his native Scandinavia...the lucky client would be thrilled beyond measure. The resort would reap a windfall of publicity. His boss would fill his coffers. And Sven would really have "made it" as a musky guide. It would be the rest of them who would elevate his status in the North Woods fishing world.

He never expressed it to anyone, but Sven was even jealous and envious of Kenny Cranston and his well-known reputation as an ardent row-troller. Kenny was taller, about six foot, and extremely well-conditioned, muscular thanks in part to his hours each day rowing his wooden rowboat on the area lakes. And despite his low-tech approach to musky fishing, Ken had gained a hard-earned reputation for bringing in some sizable trophy fish.

In some respects, he covered a good deal more water than the standard cast-and-retrieve methods everyone else employed in their fishing. He was like a perpetual motion fishing machine. Sometimes his technique was stroke, glide, wait. Stroke, glide, wait. Baits dive, wobble upward, rest momentarily. Then dive, wobble upward, and so on. Sometimes across more open and deeper water it would be a somewhat steadier, smoother, stroke, stroke, stroke - mimicking a bait fish merely swimming from one spot to another, inadvertently passing over the big, toothy, predator musky hanging a little deeper in the open water.

Kenny probably hadn't harvested as many legal muskies as were put in the boats of some of the guides over recent years, but it was possible that his average fish size was a little bit larger. His methods based on his row trolling were deliberately targeted to seek the big ones, rather than the more frequent action often sought by the guides to satisfy the desires of their clients to catch *something* with their limited time and money.

Sven envied that freedom and drive.

He was mostly glad to have his position with the resort, in part because in addition to generous tips from well-heeled clients, the resort supported him with some base salary as well...so long as the guests were happy, and they were. Besides, the resort supplied him with that boat and everything else. Some tackle and specialized equipment was his, but that was by choice. His "business expenses" and "overhead" were minimal. And that made him feel different and set apart as well.

If I could put Big Momma, that Frigg, that main goddess of the musky pantheon, in my boat, I could be free, too. His insecurity, fears, jealousy, and envy would be put to rest forever. *It would be like Asgard, and I would be on the throne.*

Chapter Five

Christine O'Malley, and don't call her "token"

Christine O'Malley never worried about being "unusual" for a female. Older relatives early on referred to her as a "tomboy." Her mother, grandmother, and aunts used to furrow brows and buzz about her lack of interest in playing with dolls or "dress up" as a frilly princess. As she grew into young womanhood, it's not that she had no desire to be "feminine." On the contrary, she possessed a natural beauty with her five-foot six-inch, graceful frame, her full, wavy blonde hair, her bright blue eyes, and dazzling smile. Christine - never "Chrissy" or just "Chris" - liked solid, outdoorsy men and knew how to be attractive when she wanted to be.

It's just that she also liked the outdoors, hunting, and fishing. She pestered her grandfather and father to take her fishing from a young age. She loved it even more than her two brothers did. Early on she proved to have more ability and success than they did, too. She took a little personal delight in regularly "out-fishing" the boys, and they hated being shown up by a girl.

Grandpa and Dad were more "generalists" when it came to their fishing. Walleyes when the spring spawning runs were on, largemouth and smallmouth bass later in the spring when the basses bedded in the shallows, a little perch, bluegill, sunfish, and other panfish for easier meals, ciscoes, or lake whitefish in the fall when they spawned over rocky underwater bars. Occasionally they cast big lures for northern pike or musky. Those toothy monsters in the pike family seemed to require a lot more time and effort than Grandpa and Dad really cared to put in most of the time.

But by the time Christine reached high school, her fishing ambitions became dominated by the fishing pinnacle of hunting trophy muskellunge. She loved to challenge herself, be it with sports, dating, work, or classes. She didn't need the aid or advice of the other anglers. She could land a musky as well as or better than any of the yahoos at the landings, bait shops, or bars.

She was initially regarded as a curiosity by many of the anglers. "You're taking your daughter out for muskies?" was a question tossed at her dad more than once when he gave in and took her out with him.

The bigger hurdle came the day she declared her career choice. She would be a professional musky guide. She knew she could do it. She'd prove doubters of her abilities wrong.

She had already gained some head-turning attention by showing up at Wayne's Bait and Tackle with a legal-sized musky a few times, and that attention became much more public when she placed third in the regional Musky Classic tournament one summer...and then actually took first the next summer!

After the tournament's positive publicity, clients found Christine. She secured her professional licensing as a registered Fishing Guide. The other pros had to accept her musky catches weren't flukes. Christine wasn't a curiosity. And having already secured her licensing as a registered Fishing Guide, it was also after that that she began to get more than a rare client booking from the sports who vacationed and weekended up in the North Woods. Her professional credibility increased, and many clients appreciated her knowledge and abilities.

But Christine knew that in some ways, acceptance at the legendary Guides Table was even a bigger mountain to scale. Thing of it was, she had no precedent to help her gain access to that exclusive, unofficial "club." There had never been a woman musky guide in the area except a fill-in for the regular staff guide was laid up for months with a broken leg. None of the other musky guides had taken her seriously, though.

"She just takes a few guests out for worm-dunking and filling a fish basket with gills and perch," Johnny had scoffed one time.

In fact, if it had been up to Johnny alone, they wouldn't have given Christine the time of day despite her accomplishments in musky hunting.

"A woman musky guide? Nonsense."

Andy liked her. And he was attracted to her.

Sven respected anyone who exhibited knowledge, skill, hard work, and results.

One night when they were all at the Table, Christine walked past with a glass of her favorite Riesling. She was chatting cheerfully with a couple of her fishing clients who were just leaving the bar.

Andy spoke up to her, "Hey Christine, we have an extra chair, pull up and join us."

Everyone else, especially curmudgeonly Johnny who visibly grimaced, would have been surprised, but truthfully, not Christine. She knew she had earned a place at one of the most specialized tables to be found anywhere on the planet.

And her chair became permanent.

Among all of the male-dominated clubs, organizations, fraternities, professions, courts, and sports...this fortress was one of the most difficult to conquer. The wall that crumbled that night, the ceiling that shattered, would have been inconceivable to most of the world, but Christine knew what she had done.

She deserved it.

But what was an even greater heresy in the professional fishing world, she had decided that there was no reason on God's green earth or in the crystal-blue water of Wigwam Lake that she shouldn't be the one to catch Big Momma. She had never even laid eyes on the gargantuan trophy, but she was determined that she would, that she would successfully get Big Momma. She would seize the crown and throne of celebrity musky guides.

She had already garnered attention from the regional television stations as "The Woman Guide among Musky Anglers," a featured spot with Hank Chalmers' "North Woods Attractions," as "the attractive musky guide," and even mention at least in a few outdoor magazine articles. Now it would be as the Champ...and despite her genial and gregarious personality, no one was going to stand in her way.

Despite her unbridled ambition, Christine genuinely was horrified at what had happened to Kenny Cranston. No, she didn't like the idea of him trying to put Big Momma in his boat. But unlike Johnny, she recognized that fishing Wigwam, and specifically fishing that particular cabbage weed-covered bar and the nearby drop-off into deeper water, was a "first come, first served" matter.

Johnny might have talked and postured like it was "his territory," and should be in some way reserved for him, but the universal, unwritten, Anglers Code was that if no one else got there first to actively fish the spot, the first person to show up had the right to work it. And to catch by legal method and keep any legal fish the fishing gods deemed to grant.

As the guides drained their glasses and got up to leave for the night, Christine said, "Well, I'm glad that at least it was an accident."

Johnny thought *Good riddance*. But didn't say it.

Sven shook his head in a gesture of regret.

Andy leaned closer to Christine and stage-whispered, "You know, we could get a nightcap at my place."

"Thanks, Andy," she smiled back, "but I have to take a party out on the chain early tomorrow morning."

She left the bar and went out to a large, back stall big enough to accommodate her old Ford 150 pickup, boat trailer, and a classic Lund 1675 Pro Guide 16-foot tiller boat with 40 hp Mercury motor. It was a solid, well-designed aluminum fishing boat with dual rod storage lockers, electronics, tackle trays, and a live box. She had bought it used but in good condition with her carefully counted pennies.

She had parked in the farthest back stall she could, and she looked at the bow of the boat as it sat on the trailer before she got in her truck.

I really have to get that dent bumped out and scrapes touched up when I have a day without clients. Sports expect their guide to maintain equipment in good, attractive condition.

Chapter Six

At Waynes' Bait and Tackle, one day later...

The next morning Christine stopped at Wayne's Bait and Tackle. Her clients for the day's fishing were repeat customers and she knew that while they would fish for muskies with a variety of lures and methods, at some point during the day they preferred to work a promising, rocky shoreline and "throw suckers."

The wide range of musky hunters or anglers all had their preferences and their theories as to what was most likely to succeed in tempting and catching the big fish. Some would cast and retrieve, cast and retrieve, over and over again, big bucktail spinner baits, twirling flashy, faceted metal blades from the head of the lure. Some swore by carved or molded, long jerk baits with the trio of treble hooks hanging from their undersides, and usually painted to suggest lake suckers, yellow perch, or even spotted trout. Some were almost addicted to casting and retrieving surface plugs with little propellers on the back, and sometimes on the front, of the lure that created wake and bubbles across the surface of the water, intended to attract the big musky to come up and strike savagely right at the surface.

And there were anglers who would put their hand on a stack of Bibles to testify that nothing, *nothing*, could beat the attraction of a real baitfish, usually a foot-long or slightly larger lake sucker, rigged with a big treble hook impaled through its body back by the tail, and another treble hook through its lips. With that rigging, often called a "harness," the theory was that if the toothy target grabbed the delicious baitfish back by its tail, or up by its head, it would likely be hooked either way.

The live bait advocates would argue - especially over whiskeys at the bar any evening - that "you just can't beat the smell, the pheromones, even the taste, of the real thing," rather than some artificial representation of a musky's meal.

So, Christine was picking up four live suckers in a big bait bucket for her sports to use if they chose to try that method. Also in the shop was Sven, paying for "two dozen scoops" of live perch minnows. His resort guests wanted fish to eat, not the highly unlikely trophy musky, so he would be taking them out on the chain of lakes to some weed beds where the yellow perch were apt to be plentiful.

The terms for the bait were misleading. According to common practice, the shop owner's "one dozen scoops" were actually quite full hand nets of thrashing minnows, not simply a dozen.

Unlike at the convenience store in town that sold live bait, where the woman proprietor would one-by-one count out an actual dozen of minnows, maybe tossing in an extra or two to appear generous, but she was considered by most to be stingy and against the accepted code of the bait business. A one dozen scoop should mean a net full. Her minnows weren't young perch fingerlings. They were small common, bluntnose, or emerald shiner, minnows, very commonly used to catch yellow perch or some other smaller fish such as crappies or walleyes.

"Sven," Christine said when she saw him. "So, you're stuck ferrying around guests for panfish today."

"Yes," he said unenthusiastically. "Whatever the customers want, so long as they pay."

"Say," she said, "have you heard anything else about the sad case of Kenny Cranston's death? And about any funeral plans or memorial service?"

If anyone knew, it'd be Sven.

"Just that the official investigation is continuing. Apparently, it's still being classified as a tragic accident. But the concern now is finding who it was who accidentally struck his boat. How it happened. And, particularly, why they fled the scene of the accident without trying to help or at least notify authorities. The prevailing theory seems to be that it was probably a vacationer or tourist who was either terrified at what they had done, or even too drunk to appreciate the seriousness of the matter. As far as a funeral or service, plans haven't been announced yet. The family is apparently considering a memorial service, whether at the Protestant church or at Shmidt's Funeral Home. I don't know yet."

"Well, be sure to pass it on if you do hear, okay?" Christine smiled gratefully. She started to turn away with her big bait bucket and the splashing live suckers but paused. "And that isn't your usual Alumacraft, is it? I didn't think it was you when I pulled up."

"No," Sven said. "The 16-footer 'musky chaser' and 40 horse motor aren't really needed today, so it's being washed and buffed up, algae removed, paint touched up on the hull, while I wrestle mightily with those perch in one of the 14-foot, shallow draft resort boats. Whatever works. Good luck today."

And for my sake, don't harass Big Momma out on Wigwam.

"You, too," Christine called back cheerily.

At least he won't be bothering Big Momma today.

Chapter Seven

Guide boat issues, five days after Kenneth Cranston's murder...

Johnny took his usual seat at the Guides Table for his brandy and assumed prominence among the professional musky fishing guides. Andy and Sven were already there with their glasses of brandy and vodka, respectively.

"John-boy," Andy said with his booming voice as the diminutive old guide sat, "so where did you fail to catch Esox muscular today?" Johnny hated the embarrassing nickname, which, of course, is why Andy poked him with it. He liked Johnny and had unspoken respect for his long record in the business, but he just had to put him down a notch or two. After all, in the end, it was a competition, and Andy would come out on top.

"Ah, it's Esox masquinongy," corrected Sven, not quite getting either joke in Andy's greeting to Johnny. On the one hand, Sven had a sense in his insecurity that he was outside or at least on the fringes of a lot of shared jokes and friendly jabs. Nonetheless he felt compelled to set the record straight on the Latin genus and species names for muskellunge. Correct information was particularly important to Sven.

Both Andy and Johnny ignored him. Johnny groused back at the giant guide. "Two follows and one half-hearted strike from an undersized fish on Warrior Lake. But at least we had some action. You do any better?"

"Nah," Andy said, but hastened to add that it was entirely due to being out of action for the day. "Had to take the *Musky Catcher* into the Marina repair shop yesterday afternoon after fishing. Damn client had to be over-helpful and try to pull the bow anchor up when I was turned away adjusting the Yamaha before moving to another location. We were anchored right on top of that rocky knob on Wigwam, casting into the drop-offs on either side. And the bow anchor had gotten stuck a bit among some of the rocks. So, this idjit yanks instead of waiting for me to swing the boat around and free it from another angle. Bangs the anchor against the fiberglass hull of the bow, making a hole. Damn tourist fisherman! Didn't seem to recognize that the bow anchor is powered by an electric motor to raise and lower it." Andy paused briefly before continuing.

"Anyway, Joe at the Marina shop has been patching and painting. Had it in there all day, drying 'til good as new. Won't even see any damage to the bow."

Sven shook his head knowingly. An inevitable complication to the guiding profession was the profusion of sports, clients, amateur anglers, who assume that they know what they are doing. They assert themselves instead of waiting for their guide's instructions. They act as though they know more about fishing than their guide does. Worst of all, they treat their guide as inferior hired help rather than rely upon their expertise.

It was virtually a mantra among the North Woods residents and professionals. "We're better off up here if you just stay 'down below' but send your money." As it was, doing business in the beautiful North Woods Lake Country was always a difficult proposition. There was no musky fishing, or need for guides, from some time in November to the following May. Some seasons the ice wasn't even off of the lakes when the new fishing season opened in May, which forced resorts to cancel most of their reservations. Fishing guides, bait and tackle shops, gift shops and souvenir stand owners, all remained idle until at least two weeks of spring weather finally showed up.

One wag was fond of saying, "Two seasons up here. Winter and July."

And the owner of the largest sporting goods store was known for his secret to making a small fortune in the North Woods, "Move up here with a large fortune."

Some resort owners and businesses closed not long after Labor Day and the fall color season that followed on its heels. A few more prosperous ones would move with the changing season to similar resorts or businesses in Southern states like Florida or Texas, returning to the North Country the following May to reopen Memorial Day weekend. It was a migration pattern that actually mimicked the Canada geese, loons, ducks, many songbirds, and even butterflies in their millennia-long travels north and south.

Others would transition to winter jobs or activities. Some merely hunkered down and waited out the inevitable 35-40 degrees below zero temperatures that deep froze the North Woods under a blanket of three or more feet of snow and ice. Snug, well-insulated homes with good, heat-efficient wood stoves and cords of well-seasoned hardwood helped folks survive the virtual hibernation.

The local bars helped, too. Of course.

During the brief fishing season, the professional fishing guides reigned with shaky supremacy over the Musky World and its lesser fishy inhabitants. That is if they could get their guide boats out on the water with paying clients.

Christine had arrived, as usual, the last to show up, but she had heard Andy speak of being out of commission that day with his boat in the shop. *And Sven had spoken about needing to swap out his customary 16-foot Alumacraft for one of the smaller resort boats. And what about Johnny?*

"Didn't I see you in your side yard, Johnny, working on your antique Adirondack?" She had driven by his place on her way to another area lake.

"Damn old boat always needs some work," he said with his usual grumble. "Nothing to talk about. Just a couple of cracked hull planks. A little patch and varnish. Nothing really."

Cracked hull planks near the bow. She puzzled. *There's always some normal wear and tear during a busy fishing season. Isn't that something he would normally defer until the off season? The daily grind of taking sports out and fishing hour after hour is more than enough, especially at his age. Well, maybe he was getting a little leakage. But if cracked that much, it would likely require more than a little "patch and varnish." Probably total replacement of plank strips. So, if "nothing really," why the rush to do it now?*

Christine never talked about it, but despite the bubbly highs, the genial and gregarious personality, the energy, and enthusiasm of her ambitious nature, she was also prone to experience "lows" that could border on depression. She was always taken by surprise when she was hit by a "down swing." And as a possible companion to the start of a low, depressed feeling, she could also experience a kind of paranoia, in which she became suspicious and mistrustful of others and their actions. She didn't self-analyze especially, so she didn't always realize that she was doing it.

But sometimes she wondered if she was suspicious without real justification. *Maybe these boat issues are entirely coincidental. Merely a convergence of bad luck in our little guides gathering. Some clients can act rashly.*

They do it all the time. Try to be too helpful. Assume they know what they are doing. Become impatient or too excited. Try to bring a big one in the net before it's sufficiently tired out. Get careless with boats and equipment.

She continued to try to think herself out of her unrealized paranoia and fringe depression, to "pull herself" back up to what she believed was her natural positive and energetic spirit. *Resorts always do maintenance and touch up the crafts in their little fleets. But during the height of the vacationing and fishing season? That's more of an off-season thing, too.*

And Johnny seemed awfully dismissive, almost secretive, about his little "patch and varnish." She felt pulled back down into her mostly unrecognized pit of suspicion. *Didn't really want to talk about it.*

Two of those unlikely scenarios, unusual coincidence. But all three? What's going on? At least one has to be "fishy." Christine didn't even think about her unintentional "punniness." Nor did she relate all of that to her own dent and scrapes. Self-reflection, analysis, and connections were not really her forte. She was more of a "go with the flow" kind of person.

But there had to be something behind a unique outbreak of boat issues.

Not nothing.

Chapter Eight

One week after Kenny's murder...

A veteran musky hunter from a Milwaukee suburb had heard the tales about Big Momma, "possibly a new world's record," the hyperbole had grown her in telling and retelling, *ad infinitum,* in fishing circles around the Upper Midwest. Big Momma wasn't nearly that big, of course, but she *was* large enough to attract a lot of attention and buzz. So, this fellow had insisted that Christine take him on Wigwam to try for her.

Christine had been engaged for several days now in a cyclical struggle within her mind to reject this "down" feeling that seemed to nibble at her psyche and emotions. Her repeat client, having fished with her several times before and being used to her "up" enthusiasm and energy, detected that she wasn't quite her outgoing self and asked if she was feeling okay.

"Oh, yah," she said. "I'm just thinking of where Big Momma is most apt to be hanging out on Wigwam at this time of day, and under these conditions. Let's go knock on her dining room door."

The morning was heavily overcast, with the possibility of rain later in the day. With no bright sun to bother the lidless eyes of the big predator fish, Christine bet that there was at least the possibility that Big Momma could be cruising near and over the tops of the cabbage weed beds on that rocky bar where she had been spotted before, and thus be relatively close to the surface, where a well-worked lure might just get her attention.

She launched the Lund guide boat at the main landing on Wigwam, parked her rig, and grabbed gear out of her truck. Which is when she noticed Andy's flashy red, double cab GMC Hummer Truck and boat trailer parked at the far end.

Damn, I hope he isn't also parked smack dab on that bar I was going to take my guy to.

But he was. Having gotten on the lake early, Andy and his two sports were working one end to the other and back again over the bar. First casting over the tops of the cabbage weed. Then throwing deep divers toward the drop-off going down to deeper water toward the middle of the lake, virtually beating the water to a froth.

Christine motored past them, careful not to rev up her motor and rudely rock Andy's slow-moving boat with her wake.

Andy looked up to see who was going by, and gleefully waved and called in her direction.

"Top of the mornin' to you, Chrissy. Better luck next time." He knew full well that both the nickname and the dig would get under her skin. Johnny wasn't the only one Andy competed against and found ways to insult. But he still wanted to date her.

Missing out on working that bar was more disappointing to her than it was to her client. He was just glad to be out fishing, hoping for at least some action if not a new world's record musky. He was especially glad to be away from his oppressive office in downtown Milwaukee.

When you're wrestling with an unseen enemy within that kept tugging you down to depression, like Christine was, even inevitable disappointments in your daily work can seem magnified. She rallied, however, and shouted to her client seated up closer to the bow.

"That's okay, there's a sharp drop-off down the shore aways where Big Momma's been spotted from time to time. No one's fishing down there. We'll try that."

The vacationing businessman gave her a thumb's up, and they sped off.

They fished the rest of the morning out on Wigwam. Along one rocky shoreline with several dead trees angled and jackstrawed out from shore into deepening water they raised a sizable musky. As it followed the lure being retrieved, it drew closer. It rose up to within inches of the surface, Christine's still down spirits also raised a bit in anticipation.

The client, meanwhile, became increasingly excited, even encouraging the fish to strike, "Come on, come on, hit it. Hit it!" But his hard-to-contain excitement also encouraged him to crank his reel handle too fast, almost yanking the lure out of the water and away from the following fish.

The musky must have rejected the ambition to become a flying fish and jump out of the water after the bait, for it slowed, almost to a stop, and then finned its way down deeper, finally disappearing with a flick of its powerful tail. The client was crestfallen, but veteran enough to know that, more often than not, that was the outcome with musky fishing. The fish of thousands and thousands of casts.

And normally Christine would have shrugged it off. After all, there were days when they didn't even raise a fish, let alone get a follow of a lure. Actual strikes were less common, hookups even less, fish actually netted or gaffed and brought into possession much less. Most outings did not result in a harvested legal musky. And it was entirely possible for an individual angler to gain a modest reputation as a successful musky catcher if he or she averaged even one legal musky a season.

Guides, of course, needed to have better production than that out of their boats to stay in business, but no one brought more than several fish to the display cases in an entire season.

By lunchtime Christine was feeling down again about both their outing and pretty much everything in general. As they motored back toward the landing, she looked over at the location of the bar they had originally hoped to fish and saw that Andy's boat was no longer working the area. The thought crossed her mind that maybe they should delay lunch and go over to try it, but a hole had opened up in the clouds overhead, and most of the surface of the lake was at least temporarily in bright sunlight. The slim chances to tie into Big Momma in the best of conditions would likely wait until evening in lower light conditions. And frankly, her energy for it was slumping.

"How 'bout we have our lunch break and then we can try again out here if you want. Maybe that fish we raised will come back near those crisscrossed logs. If it followed your lure, chances are it's feeling hungry and maybe be more aggressive."

Personally, she estimated from several years of experience guiding that it was of marginal size. Maybe 38-39 inches. Maybe, but just maybe, "stretchable" to a legal 40 inches.

Probably all of the guides, and a lot more anglers on their own, measured, one might say, "optimistically" with a fish that was really, *really* close. Even angling the tape ever so slightly over the fish from tip of snout to tip of tail might gain a fraction of an inch. Or smoothing out the tail a bit so that it projected back just a *teeny bit* more might help make the difference between being a "keeper" and a "toss it back in to grow some more."

The professional guides especially didn't want a DNR warden to show up at a landing, bait and tackle shop, or resort and catch a party with an undersized fish. In addition to citation, fine, and besmirched reputation, the result could be a license suspension for the rest of a season.

Nobody wanted that.

"Or," the client said, frankly feeling weary from a few hours of casting heavy lures with stiff musky rods, "if you don't mind, we could try over on Little Wigwam. I'm staying at the Council Fire Resort. I caught an undersized musky there once, and before I'm tuckered out from all of this casting, if you don't mind, we could fish for a few walleyes late afternoon."

Christine agreed. *It's his dollar*, she thought. *There wasn't going to be a world record, anyway.*

Chapter Nine

The same night. A narrow miss...

No muskies showed themselves on Little Wigwam, a smaller lake of about 300 acres. But about two hours before quitting time, Christine switched her client over to a lighter graphite spinning rod with eight-pound test line and a weighted jig-type lure with single hook and a feathered "skirt." When it was cast and allowed to sink over a stoney, sloping bottom, it resembled an injured minnow struggling to swim. The resemblance to this type of minnow grew when it was retrieved in short jerks, bobbing up and down in the water near the bottom. Three times 17–18-inch walleyes grabbed the jig, were hooked, fought, and netted, and put into the live well in the back of her boat.

Her client was pleased. He had gotten a good follow from a musky that *might* have been legal, and that was a thrill, and he had three fat, super-delicious walleyes for dinner one night while they were staying in their cabin at Little Wigwam.

Christine continued to struggle to be positive and encouraging to him. She wasn't sure that she felt good about accepting her fee and a nice tip, but then she really wasn't feeling good about much right then.

"You can just drop me off at the main pier on the Council Fire Resort beach," he said. "And thanks for a good outing.

We'll do it again before long. Maybe next time we'll catch the new world's record."

He smiled and waved as he climbed out of her boat, onto the pier, and walked toward his guest cabin with an inexpensive stringer and his three walleyes.

Normally she would have cleaned, field dressed, or even filleted the fish for him. Guides customarily did that messy work for clients, but he cheerfully volunteered to do that himself. It seemed to him from her demeanor that she must be tired and figured that he would let her get home for the evening.

Christine motored over to the public landing. She loaded up her Lund on her four-wheeled boat trailer by herself, towed it up the concrete ramp and into the parking lot. Then she hit the county road to head homeward.

She pondered whether she should just head straight to her modest, one-story frame house and her solitary home life - except for her big, fluffy, mixed-breed cat. She wasn't feeling up to the usual banter of the Guides Table this evening.

Johnny would be curmudgeonly as always. Andy would semi-jokingly put them down while he blustered about his abilities. Sven, well, Sven would be dour and unsure of himself.

But there *was* the imported German Riesling. *Okay, a glass might help me feel better.*

Her route to "The Fishing Hole" swung past Wigwam Lake's landing. She hardly took note of a truck and boat trailer waiting at the end of the drive. She didn't notice it pull out and follow her.

She did notice when the following vehicle flashed its bright lights and closed the distance until it hugged her back bumper. She shielded her eyes from the glare reflected by the rear-view mirror. As she glanced down momentarily at her gauges, the rig roared past.

Christine looked up, startled, as the truck veered sharply in front of her, its rear lights and its trailer lights shining red and bright like stop lights. It swung in front of her, almost hitting the front left bumper and fender of her aging pickup truck.

She jerked her steering wheel to the right to miss what looked like it was going to be an impact, and she caught the gravel berm of the county road with her right front wheel. Her boat nearly jackknifed as the trailer skidded into the softer soil alongside the road. She fought to correct the problem, but the trailer's tires sank into the soft wet dirt as she came to a stop.

Christine unhitched the trailer with a small hand crank.

It's so dark. Those bright headlights were way-y to close. Almost blinded me.

She pushed it as straight as possible, parallel to the road.

Was it a black truck? I couldn't tell.

She re-hitched the trailer.

Was that Johnny? He has a black truck.

She got back in her truck.

He knew that I was taking a sport on Wigwam today.

She put the truck in the lowest gear.

He's so jealous about Big Momma. He thinks she's his.

Christine checked for approaching vehicles.

He really hates it that we all know about Big Momma and try for her when we can.

As she eased back onto the road, Christine wondered aloud, "But would he cause an accident?"

Christine's suspicious streak and issues with paranoia welled up quite uncontrollably.

Then there's Andy. In low light conditions red can look like black. Even with his jabbing humor earlier today at that rocky bar, he really doesn't like anyone competing for Big Momma.

Christine's train of thought alternated between an internal track to a spoken one. "He says he wants to go out with me, but..."

There's nothing Andy wants more than catching a fifty pounder.

"That's more important to him than dating me."

Or his relationships with the other guides at the Table. Or just about anything else.

"But would he value it more than human life?"

And Sven? Well, Sven would like to put Big Momma in his boat just like the rest of us, but he's too uptight and strait-laced to resort to trying to eliminate competition for her.

"Or is he?"

He's stubborn and stern.

At that point she remembered poor Kenny Cranston. "What if his fatal accident wasn't an accident at all?"

What if he was getting too close to hooking Big Momma and was taken out before he succeeded? His methods were laborious but effective. I can picture several guides really chafing if some mere fisherman harvested that elusive fifty pounder. Even I didn't appreciate his work on Wigwam's cabbage weed bar.

"Or could it be someone else?"

And if it could be, who? And why? We know most of the Wisconsin Musky Club avid musky chasers. But some average Joe Fisherman? Or, or...

At that point, shaken and exhausted by her workday and her harrowing experience, Christine was incapable of sorting out what was actually possible, what was likely, what was worth devoting thoughts and actions to...from what was no more than suspicion and paranoia beyond reason.

She drove on to the big parking lot of "The Fishing Hole" and marched into the bar, to the Guides Table. Despite her typical cheerful greetings, her emotions continued to slide toward suspicion and depression.

Is one of them out to get me?

Chapter Ten

The next day, an investigation broadens...

Fortunately, Christine had the next morning open. A client had booked with her later in the day, after lunch, for what was known as a "Half-day Outing." He was a casual fisherman who preferred to sleep in and spend a few hours before nightfall trying to bag an elusive musky. "Half-days" cost a sport about forty per cent less than a full day's outing, and thus were at least a little more economical than wearing yourself out all day long casting those long, stiff rods and weighty lures.

The larder was looking pretty empty since she had been too busy to make it into Mary's Grocery to restock her fridge and freezer, so Christine opted to stop for a walleye sandwich and coffee at Fisherman's Cafe. Besides, she was also low on coffee, and they would fill her big thermos with strong, dark, hot coffee for $3.99, taking care of her, and this half-day angler, for the entire afternoon. She also loaded up on candy and energy bars to share with him.

The breaded deep-fried walleye sandwich was delicious, a sizable filet that lapped out of the big bun, with lettuce, sliced tomato, and tasty tartar sauce. Showing some restraint, and mindful of her waistline, she passed on the basket of French fries that they included in the combo order. There were always enough fries to feed two or three people.

Thermos in hand, she headed out to the spacious parking lot toward her truck and boat, and immediately saw Sven parked alongside her rig. He was talking to a uniformed DNR fish and game warden, a Wisconsin State Patrol officer in uniform, and a man in plain clothes with a clip board and some fragments in his hand. Sven had his spruced-up 16-foot Alumacraft back on his boat trailer, and while the men were gesturing toward his boat, she couldn't help but notice that they were looking over at the bow of her Lund as well.

That pesky paranoia and sinister suspicion welled up again from deep in her emotions.

"What's going on, guys?" Christine asked as casually as she could muster.

"There's an investigation going on, Christine," Sven said, but the highway patrol officer was quick to reply.

"Good afternoon, ma'am," he said, with a slight tip of his broad-brimmed trooper's hat. "I'm Sergeant Williams, and this is Dr. Alexander from the Wisconsin State Crime Laboratory in Madison."

The middle-aged man, dressed in a sport coat and tie, clutched a clipboard and a bag marked "evidence" that held some jagged fragments. He nodded politely but seemed mostly preoccupied with peering at the bow of her boat.

"May we ask you a few questions?" the trooper said.

"Ah, well sure," she replied. "But first may I ask again, what's going on here? Am I under suspicion for something?"

Nervous and insecure as he often was, Sven spoke up out of turn. "Oh no, no, they told me that they're just conducting an informal fact-gathering, ah, geez, ah..."

Trooper Williams held up his hand to stop him politely. "Allow me to explain. The preliminary conclusion in the investigation of Kenneth Cranston's death over a week ago on Wigwam Lake is that he suffered a tragic, fatal accident. The primary concern at this point is that whoever struck his boat and caused his fatal injury fled the scene of the accident without reporting it. They also did not stay to assist or provide vital information as to just what happened and how it happened. Depending upon a variety of factors, the driver of the other boat and any companion could be charged with felony 'hit and run,' or at least a misdemeanor. In either case, it's a serious matter, and we are following up on that unknown suspect and boat.

"You should know that what has happened to date is that after a thorough canvassing, we've put together a list of boats and owners who have been observed by eyewitnesses on Wigwam Lake in the past two weeks. And while this listing is not considered complete, Mr. Karlsson here, and you, and your state-registered boats have been seen on Wigwam during that period. No one is subject to arrest at this point. This is merely fact-finding. Do you agree that you and your boat have been on the lake in the last two weeks?"

"Well, ah, sure, I've taken a couple of clients out there in that period. Ah, do you need a subpoena to examine my boat? Do I need legal representation? I'm not sure of my legal rights..."

Before she could complete her own questions, Dr. Alexander turned and stated matter-of-factly, "No, not this Lund. The dent and scrapes show very small bits of granite dust in the scratches. And the impact is suggestive of a rounded but jagged rock. Plus," he concluded as he held up the fragments in his hand, "there's no paint or varnish specks that would match these pieces."

It was then that both Christine and Sven realized that the lab analyst was holding small remnants of Kenny Cranston's rowboat.

Sergeant Williams turned back to Christine.

"To answer your questions, ma'am, no. A subpoena is not needed to look at your boat here as it's parked in a public lot, available for view by any passerby. It would be a different matter if we needed to go on your private property or gain access to it in your private garage or shed."

Christine exhaled a breath that she hadn't realized she was holding.

The State Police Sergeant continued, "As for legal representation, you are always accorded and protected in your right to obtain legal counsel when you so decide and request. But again, no one is under arrest or detention here. And we have no further questions of you. Thank you for your cooperation. We'll bid you good day."

Christine noted that Dr. Alexander scribbled some notes and made a couple of check marks on his clipboard sheets.

The sergeant turned to Sven, however, and commented, "It's obvious Mr. Karlsson that your resort's Alumacraft boat that you are using has very recently been buffed and cleaned at the bow. We may need to subpoena the boat from its owner to examine more deeply what lies in the metal under the maintenance and buffing. We'll be in touch with him."

Sven, by nature a worrier, blurted, "You mean I'll lose use of my boat again? What about my client and guest bookings? For how long would you have it? Oh, this is horrible. The gods are against me. Oh, oh..."

Christine reached out and put what she hoped was a steadying hand on Sven's arm. Despite her own struggle with depressive feelings, she felt sorry for the dour Swede. She knew, as did he, that the resort would supply him with a smaller, shallower draft 14-footer, but it wasn't nearly as serviceable or properly equipped for his guiding needs.

He hated himself for feeling that way, but he also couldn't help but feel a poorly placed jealousy of Christine. Although delusional, Sven felt duped by Christine, as though she'd gained an unfair advantage over him. If he didn't know better, he'd think she'd been praying to, and won favor from, his beloved gods Frigg or Njord for them not to favor him, but her.

How will I be equipped as I need to be in order to capture Big Momma? This is terrible, he thought. He envied the others at the Guides Table. It was not nearly as disastrous as he was making it out to be, but no one could have convinced him of that.

Sven was definitely not a "go with the flow," adjust and adapt kind of guy.

Chapter Eleven

*And broadens some more,
that evening and the next day...*

That evening, mere hours after Christine and Sven's encounter with the authorities outside the Fisherman's Cafe, the usual suspects, not that they would have appreciated the term at that point, sat at the Guide's Table.

Christine was feeling somewhat better by then. She didn't know why she was experiencing an upswing emotionally. But she was encouraged that she and her boat were not currently being investigated regarding the death of Kenny Cranston.

Not that she had ever thought that she should be.

Sven, however, was more "down" than even his usual reserve and worry. He nervously swirled his favorite vodka around and around in his glass, in a frankly disquieting kind of way, staring down much of the time. When asked about the experience outside Fisherman's Cafe earlier that day, he was glumly terse, and less informative than he normally would be.

Andy pressed him a bit, "What have you heard, Sven? Is this merely a matter of the authorities trying to track down somebody who fled the scene of an accident without reporting it or trying to help? Or do they suspect foul play. Somebody who had it in for Kenny?"

They had gotten quite used to his natural penchant for knowing all kinds of facts and information.

"All I know is they want to seize my boat," he said glumly. "Like the sergeant said, the preliminary call is accidental death. If they have other suspicions, they are staying mum about it." He went back to swirling his drink around and staring down at it, as though mesmerized by the swishing liquor.

"But who would be so hateful toward Kenny that they would want to crash his rowboat and maybe even murder him in the process?" Christine asked. "Do we know if he drowned? Or suffered fatal injury?"

That much Sven did know. He broke his silent brooding and worry enough to say, "Skull fracture and massive head trauma. Dead before he could drown." More swirling and swishing.

"Still say he asked for it," Johnny didn't care how cruel or uncaring that sounded. "He shouldn't have been fishing that spot."

He knew better, of course. "First come, first served" was the code for everyone when it came to fishing spots in public waters. But he still believed in grand, exalted fashion that *he* should have priority in fishing for Big Momma. All of his years, all of his hard, grueling work, all of his past successes and contributions to the sport of musky hunting. *He* was the one who deserved the crowning glory of the rare fifty-pounder.

Christine couldn't help but shake her head at his more than curmudgeonly attitude. *For God's sake, Kenny had a family. He worked hard and long for his angling accomplishments.* She respected and appreciated the patriarchy of Johnny's position among North Woods musky guides, but his callous disregard for Kenny's demise was hard to take.

Andy, of course, disagreed from his own perspective. "Don't matter to me that he was fishing that bar for Big Momma. He was just wasting his time and effort," he blustered. "I'm gonna get her with my superior skill and methods!" He leaned back in his chair and chortled, laughing so hard that his beer belly bounced his suspenders.

Johnny shot him his signature glare. *Damned showboat.* He still had a liking for Andy. It was hard not to. But that trophy of a lifetime was still meant to be *his*.

The following day the investigation widened to both of the Mutt and Jeff duo. The same investigation team of Sergeant Williams and Dr. Alexander flagged down Johnny just as he was about to get into his black Chevy Silverado and leave his driveway towing his antique Adirondack guide boat.

The unmarked state trooper's car stopped in front of the four-door Silverado, blocking its exit. Sergeant Williams got out and cordially addressed Johnny.

"Sir, a moment please."

Johnny immediately knew what it was about and felt indignant that he would have to be questioned in their sham investigation.

Don't they know my standing and importance in the professional musky guide ranks?

He drew himself up to the full height of five foot five inches and sniffed. "You want to examine my boat? *My* boat? I trust you know to whom you are speaking."

"Yes sir," the state trooper said. "We're merely gathering information and facts. This will only take a minute of your time."

"Go ahead," he harrumphed. "Damn waste of time." He meant *his* time. He couldn't care less about some damn state public employee's time.

While the sergeant was speaking with Johnny, the forensic analyst was already scrutinizing the repairs recently done to the bow of Johnny's boat.

"It's not entirely clear," Dr. Alexander said. "While there's no trace of the rowboat hull fibers on this Adirondack, these front plank strips have been replaced or patched, so that may have eliminated impact evidence. On the other hand, there are no varnish specks from the Adirondack on these rowboat fragments. Not clear."

"You mean my boat wasn't involved," Johnny spat indignantly. "Now let me pass, I have more important things to get on with."

"Have a nice day, sir," Sergeant Williams said with his customary touch to his wide hat brim. "We may need to talk to you again before long. Don't leave your guide boat anywhere outside of our local area."

The two of them got back in the unmarked car and pulled away.

Johnny also pulled out to go pick up his client for the day.

This crap sure as hell puts a damper on an otherwise promising day to chase muskies.

His sport had no idea why, but Johnny's usual curmudgeonly, no-nonsense mood was darker for the rest of the day. Even darker than the heavy overcast that should bring the big fish up closer to the surface of the waters.

Andy, on the other hand, proactive and forward as always, saved the investigators the trouble of finding him and his boat. He happened to drive past Johnny's house and yard just as they were leaving. He guessed their identity and waved them down. Both the investigators and Andy pulled into the roadside rest area only a few hundred yards east of Johnny's house.

"Thought you might like to talk to me and take a gander at my boat," he boomed as they approached each other. "Might as well save you the trouble of having to look for me. Besides, I need to pick up my client and take him over to Wigwam Lake for the day...or as long as it takes us to catch Big Momma." Andy never had any lack of competitive drive.

"And," he rolled on without hesitation, "you'll note that the Marina did some patch and refinishing near the bow recently. Stupid amateur fisherman banged the hull with my bow anchor, made a hole."

"We appreciate your cooperation, Mr. Nash," Sergeant Williams said respectfully. "We'll be out of your way shortly. This is Dr. Alexander from the State Forensics Lab."

Dr. Alexander nodded slightly in Andy's direction but hurried to look at the repaired section and the rest of the bow of his Skeeter "bass boat."

Completely unconcerned about what the state lab rat was doing, Andy boomed on. "You a fisherman, Sergeant Williams? I bet a hard-nosed state trooper like you would chase muskies, head straight for the ultimate trophy."

"I cast around for bass and walleyes a little when on family vacations," the state police sergeant replied. "Can't say that I ever had the time and all of the hours of work to put into musky fishing."

"Well, you should," Andy smilingly encouraged him. "You seem like a top-of-the-line kind of guy." It was hard not to like Andy, despite his over-the-top personality.

"Doesn't look like this boat, either," said the analyst. "There are no minuscule red fibers scraped off on these fragments of the rowboat, but maybe we should check the fragments of fiberglass removed at the Marina shop to clean up the hole for patching."

"Well check to your heart's delight," Andy smiled broadly. "Talk to Joe. He's the shop boss and worked on my boat. Don't waste your time talking to either of his assistants. They don't know much. Oh, and there should be edge of the hole fragments either in their trash bin or even on the floor of the shop. They only get rid of debris once a week, and that won't be until next Monday, after the busy weekend."

A lot of people would probably think that Andy was *too* cooperative and forthcoming, but it just wasn't in his nature to play anything close to the vest, fishing or otherwise.

His proactiveness could also be disarming, however, and Sergeant Williams couldn't help but leave him with, "Thank you again, Mr. Nash, for making yourself and your boat available. We probably won't need to bother you again."

Andy, Christine, and Sven sat at the Guides Table again that evening. Each started to share their own encounters with the investigators and where things seemed to be going with looking into the death of Kenny Cranston.

"Has anyone seen Johnny?" Christine wondered. "He's usually here by now."

"Yah," Andy said. "Not only is he getting older and slowing down these days, but he doesn't like to put in such long, grueling days anymore. Time to pass the mantle and give up the crown," he joked.

Sven was feeling somewhat better this evening. The investigators hadn't gotten around to requesting or subpoenaing his 16-foot Alumacraft from the resort, so he used it in his guiding.

"Oh, I think Johnny's coming in now."

Despite his small stature, Johnny could be seen through the milling bar crowd, which made way for him, his sport, and a very wet, frankly slimy, legal-size musky. The old guide plopped the dead fish smack dab down on the hardwood floor alongside the bar, not bothering to clear away scattered peanut shells and escaped kernels of popcorn.

The barkeep didn't mind. This kind of dramatic action drew attention to "The Fishing Hole." In fact, some tourists decided not to leave when Johnny and his client hoisted the big fish by its gill plate to keep its tail from dragging on the ground. They followed fish and fishermen in to hear all about it.

A teenage young man with his family squeezed his way through the crowd to get an unobstructed view of the musky, shimmering in the neon lights of the bar, with its olive-green sides and its pattern of wavy bars in its coloration. And you couldn't miss those long, sharp teeth jutting up and down from its big jaws.

"There, by God in heaven," Johnny proclaimed loud enough for everyone present to hear, "who says I don't have it in me anymore?!" He was both bombastic and slightly out-of-breath in his excited vindication and triumph.

"How big?" a patron asked.

"Hey, that's a four-footer, easy," said another amateur fisherman and drinker.

In truth, it was just barely the 40-inch minimum size, but a bigger fish than almost all of the people present had ever caught, or even seen. Johnny's face gleamed with delight at retaking his rightful throne among the professional musky guides. He wiped sweat from his brow as he accepted offers from patrons to buy him and his client drinks. Johnny's grandiosity eclipsed the probably once-in-a-lifetime achievement of the client who actually caught the musky, but the client didn't mind. He contemplated the mounted trophy he'd hang above his mantle at home.

Johnny finished his congratulatory drinks, patted his client on the back, and excused himself to claim his customary chair at the Guides' Table.

His colleagues congratulated him, and Christine asked, "Where'd you harvest that fish?"

Out in the milling crowd there had been more than one who asked as people always do, "Where'd ya catch it?" But traditionally, successful musky catchers tended to be coy and evasive about exactly where they caught a big one. Very often they would identify the lake, especially if it was going to be a matter of record, but almost never the precise spot on the body of water.

It was slightly foolish, truth be known, since there was very little chance that anyone else could rush out to that very location on a particular lake and catch another big one. It *was* possible that a particular rocky bar, that same drop-off from shallow into deeper water, those same tangled logs or lush weed beds, were such desirable feeding grounds for trophy fish that sooner or later another "big one" would be hanging around there. But it was unlikely to an extreme that someone could soon catch the fish of a lifetime in exactly the same spot. Nonetheless, anglers and guides just didn't like to divulge "their" places of success.

In fact, it was very common for the successful musky catcher simply to lie about the whole "where" matter. To name the wrong lake, or at least the wrong place on the lake.

For one thing, a widespread myth among the anglers and guides was the belief in a "hot" lake or body of water. Rarely, and usually for rather mysterious reasons, a particular body of water could seem to "turn on" and become more productive from a fish-catching standpoint. But that almost never happened in musky hunting. Almost never, for instance, was more than one legal-size musky caught on a particular lake in any one day, and most days none would be.

And Johnny held to all of those traditions and beliefs. To "where did you harvest it?" he replied to his fellow guides,

"Oh, on the chain." And that included hundreds and hundreds of acres of water spread among several connected lakes. He might as well have said, "in a lake." But for John Jenkins, what had started out as a dark, damped-down day ended as a day of restoration in his mind and psyche.

He was back on top...not that he had ever abdicated.

Chapter Twelve

The next night at the Guides Table...

Christine arrived at the Guides Table expecting to be last as usual. Johnny was there. But neither Sven nor Andy had arrived. She gratefully took her glass of German Riesling, sipped, and then asked if Johnny knew of their whereabouts.

"Doesn't surprise me much," he said in his curmudgeonly manner, "but there's been a scandal in our little club."

Christine reacted with an alarmed look. "Scandal? What scandal? Oh, surely neither of them was the one who crashed into Kenny's rowboat! Did the investigation sweep one of them up?"

"No, not that," he replied. "You know that there was an annual Musky Rodeo tournament over on the Turtle-Flambeau Flowage this past weekend?"

"Yah," she said, "but I didn't put a boat or clients into it. I had a regular who missed a legal fish strike last season, and he keeps wanting to go back to the same area on Warrior Lake to see if lightning will strike again. It didn't by the way. But what about the Rodeo event? And what do you mean, scandal?"

Johnny was usually spare with his words as well as often grumpy, but it became obvious that this particular subject had him worked up.

"Now I didn't go over to the damn 'Rodeo' either. Hate those fussy tournaments, restricting you to what water you can fish on so as not to crowd any one lake, all the crowds, amateur anglers, showman stuff. Pain in the ass." He paused and raised an eyebrow.

"But our guy did. And got caught 'weighting' a fish." He was referring to the dishonest practice of jamming some weight down a captured musky's throat and into its stomach to make it weigh more than it should. Just about all fishing tournaments - bass, walleyes, as well as muskies - ranked contestants and awarded prizes according to weight on registered scales at the end of the fishing time on the final day.

Concerned about his absence, Christine gasped, "Oh, not Sven, I hope. He's been feeling really down lately, and insecure about how things were going for him."

"No. Your boyfriend. Andy," Johnny groused. It was hard to tell which feeling was greater on his part - the disgust that one of their number would cheat in that way, or the perverse delight that the "Paul Bunyan of guides" got what was coming to him.

The damn showman.

Andy wasn't Christine's boyfriend. She let that one go, wanting to find out the details about what had happened.

"He's hyper competitive, we all know that," she said. "But I find it hard to believe that he would try to cheat like that. That could be fatal to his guiding career, and he values that way-y more than a shiny trophy and some cash prize at a weekend tournament."

Johnny harrumphed as usual, "Maybe you don't know him as well as you think." But at that moment Sven showed up.

She turned to him as he sat down with his vodka.

"Johnny and I were just talking about the cheating that went on at the Turtle-Flambeau last weekend. I guess Andy was involved. You know anything about that?"

Also as usual, Sven did. "I was there, taking a resort guest out to participate. According to Andy, he and his sport succeeded in putting a legal musky in his live well to register in the tournament on that last day, Sunday at 3:00. There were only five legal fish taken during the whole time from Friday evening to mid-Sunday afternoon. The winning fish went 43 inches and a solid twenty pounds..."

"Too much information, Sven," Christine chided him good-naturedly. "What about this charge of Andy cheating?"

"Well, according to Andy himself, his client's fish was weighed on a hand-held scale in the boat after netting at sixteen pounds, seven ounces. That would make it fourth out of the five, just missing the third-place trophy and cash prize of $300. The fish standing at third and in the money was weighed at sixteen pounds, twelve ounces, barely five ounces ahead of Andy's client."

"So?" Christine motioned for him to get on with it.

"So, again according to Andy, everyone was riveted on the weigh-in of the third-place fish, including Andy. The lucky fisherman and guide were posing with their fish hanging on the scale, cameras and camera phones clicking, newspaper photographers firing off flashes. And while Andy had his back turned on his sport and their fish in the live well..."

"Yes, yes..." Christine was caught up in the dramatic telling of the incident.

"...well, he claims that the fellow reached into the big tackle box, snuck out three three-ounce lead weights, and forced them down the musky's gullet while no one was looking over at their boat."

"Well," Christine said, "nine ounces of lead weights wouldn't make much of a noticeable lump at the surface of the belly of a fish of that size. How did they catch the cheating?"

"Andy probably bungled it," Johnny grumbled.

"Come on, Johnny," she said. "Let him finish. And give some benefit of the doubt to Andy."

Sven wrapped up his story and what he had actually observed in person, standing nearby at the time. "Whoever was truly responsible - let's say it was Andy's client - was rushing to get the lead weights inserted quickly before anyone could see what he was doing. The last one was not shoved down far enough into the musky's throat, and once their fish was weighed and pronounced the new third place fish, the landing judge for the tournament lifted it off of the hanging scale, the fish slipped out of his hand and flopped on the pier, and the third weight squirted out. The others were quickly discovered."

The listening guides shook their heads, not wanting to believe what they were hearing.

"A big hubbub ensued, Andy, his sport, and their fish were disqualified, of course. Some law enforcement and/or legal action could result. Andy could have his guide's license revoked or suspended."

"That's horrible," Christine said. "I don't know if Andy was complicit or to blame in any way, but you have to feel badly for him. And it certainly doesn't reflect well on our whole 'fraternity' of professional fishing guides."

"That's for damn sure," Johnny said. "This may not be as bad as Kenny Cranston's death, but I sure don't need this."

"Speaking of which," Christine said with furrowed brow, "I wonder what, if anything, is happening with that investigation."

Chapter Thirteen

Emerson Winthrop Adams III
Two weeks after Kenneth Cranston's Murder...

The slow, methodical, seemingly unproductive investigation of who had caused Kenny Cranston's death and what boat was involved continued at its dogged pace. With no witnesses who had come forward or been identified through the canvassing, the same effort continued to identify what boats and persons had been seen on Wigwam Lake in the two weeks or so prior to his fatal "accident." It was a process of making a list, however uncertain, and one-by-one eliminating each from suspicion or possibility.

Although the investigators hadn't taken Sven's boat, neither Sven nor the other Guides were considered suspects. Detectives compiled a list of all the well-known fishing clubs, Musky Hunters clubs, and well-known participants in the sport. They paid particular attention to anyone who could possibly have a grudge or objection to Kenny being so zealous about trying to catch Big Momma or "hog" prime fishing spots on Wigwam.

Everyone knew that coming up with a strong suspect was the proverbial "shot in the dark," but a new theory had arisen that perhaps it was not an accidental collision between two boats. Interestingly enough, it was Christine's "down period" worrying and suspicions that had given some lift to this "not so accidental" line of speculation. She had expressed some of her paranoia and worrisome reasoning from time to time to others. Deep laboratory analysis with sophisticated testing had resulted in a model that started to "fit" with Christine's thoughts. For one thing, it was determined from the impact point on the wreck of Kenny's boat that he had been struck at close to a 90-degree angle, the bow of the striking boat crashing directly into the side planking of Kenny's. Analysis also modeled a high rate of speed. And the direction of the "attacking" boat was highly significant. The slightly curving underwater bar covered with its lush cabbage weed was long and paralleled the shoreline only about 100 feet, plus or minus, offshore.

It was gauged highly unlikely that any boat traveling at a high rate of speed would "accidentally" strike Kenny's rowboat while moving head-on directly toward shore. A line of travel more or less parallel to Kenny's, in effect sideswiping him, maybe. But this was analyzed to have a 95 per cent chance of being deliberate, within standard deviation models.

Kenny was almost certainly targeted and murdered, and his killer was someone who was familiar with boating and/or fishing on Wigwam Lake.

That evening was the tragic two-week "anniversary" of Kenneth Cranston's murder. All but Sven were seated with their drinks at the Guide's Table. Johnny and Christine didn't have to bother to ask Andy about his "cheating scandal" at the Musky Rodeo tournament.

"About those lead weights shoved down the gullet of my client's musky out on the flowage," Andy said with his usual forwardness and gusto. "I'm exonerated." He beamed and a wide smile broke out above his bushy, brown-red beard. And in a signature move he stuck both thumbs under his suspenders and gave them a self-satisfied little "snap."

"Really?" said Christine, genuinely happy for him, and to be honest, for all of them.

"Yup," Andy said. "Both a DNR fish and game warden and a county deputy sheriff questioned my client and me, separately, of course, so that we couldn't synchronize our stories. And the Director of the Musky Rodeo tournament was there, too. Well, I truly hate to say it, but my guy folded with the pressure. He admitted that he had done it on his own, that I had no part or knowledge of what he had done. He was almost in tears making the excuses that he merely wanted for once in his fishing life to be known for catching not only his first legal musky, but a prize-winner in a fishing tournament as well. He didn't even care so much about the trophy and the cash, or the 'glory' of it all. He just wanted to be able to brag to his family, friends, neighbors, and coworkers. Plus, to have the mount and a fancy plaque on his office wall."

Andy shook his head as he said, "Shame about not placing in the tournament's final rankings. But I'll get 'em next time." He beamed.

Johnny harrumphed.

Sven rushed in, gasping for breath, his usual reserve abandoned. "What'd I miss? What were you guys talking about?"

Christine started to answer, "Well..." But before she could get another word out, Andy jumped in.

"I'm exonerated. Innocent of all charges. Didn't win, place, or show at the tournament finals, but I'll get 'em next time."

"Didn't need to repeat," Johnny grumbled almost under his breath.

"Great. Glad for you," Sven said, but quickly changed topics before Andy could continue his self-congratulatory momentum. "And do I have news!" It was a remarkable burst of enthusiasm for Sven. If Johnny was the physical opposite of Andy, Sven had to be the personality opposite.

"Do go on," Christine responded. "What's up?"

"It's the Kenny Cranston case," Sven dove right into it. "They've made an arrest."

"Really?" Christine widened her eyes.

"No fooling?" Andy boomed. "So, who was it? What's the charge?"

Sven addressed the second question first. "According to my friend in the Sheriff's Department, probably second-degree murder. It could be elevated to first-degree murder if the prosecutor determines that there was preconceived intention of killing. But intentions are difficult to nail down. Defense will surely argue that the defendant was angry, but that while he wanted to strike at Kenny for some justifiable reason, he really didn't intend to kill him. And this defendant can afford some pretty high-level defense counsel."

"So, you still haven't said *who*," Christine pressed, "and the suspense is killing me. Sorry, poor choice of words."

Sven went on. "Emerson Winthrop Adams, the Third, to be precise. Here's the gist. This Emerson Adams, III, is the descendant of some historical New England families, extremely entitled, wealthy, self-important to the max, and a successful commodities trader on the CBOE in Chicago. So, he and his wife, also a wealthy socialite, have this luxurious vacation home on Wigwam Lake. They spend frequent weekends and summer vacations up here."

Sven paused briefly, still catching his breath.

"So, Emerson Winthrop spends a lot of his time in this fancy summer home doing what he does in his workaholic life down in Chicago. He works on his computer online, on the phone, wheeling and dealing. He's not about to take much time to do such frivolous activities as swimming, lying in the hammock, or, God forbid, fishing."

All eyes and ears remained focused on Sven as he continued.

"He doesn't care one whit about musky hunting. For him it's too labor-intensive, time-consuming, almost always unproductive. So, the investigation discovered that he sets a couple of expensive, carbon-graphite spinning rods in stake rod holders on his pier and casts out a weighted hook with a nightcrawler. He lets it dangle below a red and white bobber in the water. Then he goes up to his desk in his big study. Every so often, he finishes some work he's doing and grabs a pair of binoculars. He looks out the big picture window to check on his bouncing bobbers. If one or both of them have disappeared below the surface, he goes down and picks up the rod to crank in some walleye or northern pike, or whatever fish has hooked itself."

Johnny scoffed, "Damned cheater."

"Not only is it highly unethical, downright despicable, and illegal, it's dangerous. By not keeping his lines under direct vision and control all of the time he's 'fishing,' he makes a hazard by having these long, mostly invisible lines extending out from his pier. Which is how Kenny came to be, well, entangled with this entitled, privileged, you-know-what."

They all nodded, knowing what maternal slur he was hinting at.

"About twilight on the night of his death, Kenny was row-trolling his double lures past this big shot's pier. Well, out from the end of it. He wouldn't have been able to see the virtually invisible monofilament lines cast way out toward the center of the bay. One of Kenny's lures must have gotten hooked and entangled with the guy's line. Not knowing any better in the fading light, Kenny assumed a musky had struck his lure. So, he grabbed that rod and gives it a hearty 'set,' raring back and cranking his reel."

The bartender brought Sven his vodka. Sven nodded his thanks and went on.

"The force of what he thought was 'setting the hook' yanked the expensive rod and reel right out of the rod holder on the guy's pier. He towed it into the water. Kenny soon realized that he didn't have a fish on the end of his line. So, he reeled in, came to the hooked nightcrawler and bobber combination. He logically assumed that he'd tangled with someone's broken off fishing line. He cut it free, reset his line, lure, and rod, and continued his trolling down the length of the bay. Goodbye $400 rod and reel combo."

Sven took a quick sip of his vodka.

"While this was happening, it seems that the rich, self-important commodities trader was looking out with his binoculars. He saw Kenny's rowboat, his empty rod holder, and jumped to the conclusion that Kenny didn't like him fishing off his own pier. Entitled and privileged, he figured that he should 'own' rights as far as he can cast out into the water off his pier. He blew his top over losing what might amount to less than one percent of one of his commissions."

Andy shook his head in disgust. "Money loves money."

"So, Emerson Adams III threw down his binoculars, grabbed his jacket, and ran furiously down to his pier where he had his expensive Mastercraft X-7 water ski boat tied up alongside the pier. He jumped in, started up his inboard motor, and roared off to find the bastard who lost his rod and reel in the depths."

Sven took a deeper gulp of the vodka.

"By this time, Kenny had rowed around to the cabbage weed-covered rocky bar where Big Momma had been seen a few times..."

Johnny interrupted, "That's where I've followed her. And it's where I'm going to catch her," exerting his own presumption of importance and privilege.

"Not if I get her first," Andy boomed, delighted to needle the old guide.

Undiscouraged, Sven continued and wrapped up his account of Kenny's tragic demise. "So, Kenny was row-trolling along the bar, and probably really focused on what he figured was his best chance of tying into Big Momma. Maybe he didn't even look up at the ski boat bearing directly for his mid-hull. Too late to try to evade the collision, he might have turned toward the loud noise approaching him. But Emerson crashed into him, smashing right through the wooden rowboat, propelling poor Kenny into the water. The ski boat must have also struck Kenny in his head, cracking his skull, possibly even killing him before he could drown."

"Wow," Christine gasped in genuine horror. "And all over a spinning rod and reel."

"Well, probably more to the point," Sven said, "An enraged, out-of-control reaction to what Emerson regarded as an offense against his presumption of status and, again, privilege."

Even Andy dropped his usual hearty smile and attitude and shook his head at the senselessness of the incident.

Johnny grimaced sternly and looked down, feeling sorry for what happened, perhaps for the first time since the news of Kenny's death was announced.

Finally, after a few seconds of what amounted to mournful silence, Andy spoke up again and asked Sven, "So, do you know how the authorities figured out all of that?"

"According to my deputy sheriff friend," said Sven, "it seems that their slow, methodical canvassing of boats observed on Wigwam over the two weeks before the murder also extended to cottage and boat owners on the lake itself. They obtained a subpoena to examine Emerson's ski boat. He had parked it in the old boathouse on his shoreline and hadn't even bothered to have the scrapes and wood fibers from Kenny's boat cleaned off his bow."

"Bastard probably figured why go to the expense of wiping a bug smear off until he was ready to put it into storage for the winter," Christine said.

151

"The shame of it all," Sven added, "is that with the best defense attorneys money can buy, who knows what consequences, if any, Emerson Winthrop Adams III will ever have to bear. The legal maneuvering and court appearances will likely go on into next year, maybe the next. They'll throw up so many arguments and motions and legal smoke screen that, who knows, maybe he'll end up ducking any jail time whatsoever."

"I can testify to that," Andy said. "I suffered a burglary some years back. Guy was caught. Guilty as charged. They had him dead to rights. Judge sentenced him, ordered financial restitution to be made to me. Even an overworked public defender tied the process up so much that I had to return to court *seven times* to get the restitution order finalized and on paper. Talk about broken systems."

"Well, it's good to know that all of us are off the hook and free of that pesky investigation," Christine smiled, feeling more "up" again.

Even curmudgeonly Johnny agreed. "I'll drink to that," he said, lifting his glass.

"And to poor Kenny," Christine added. "May he row-troll across perfect musky water in God's heavenly kingdom."

"And finally have the spirit of Big Momma lifted into his boat," Andy boomed.

Johnny didn't agree with that.

Chapter Fourteen

That same evening, as dusk faded into darkness on Wigwam Lake...

No boats. No guide boats, fishing boats, or ski boats. No one cruised the long, curving cabbage weed bar on Wigwam Lake.

No one except Big Momma.

The giant muskellunge glided smoothly and silently along the tops of the cabbage weed. She brushed some of the aquatic plants as she finned like a live submarine through the dark water. It was getting later in the summer season, and already she packed away thicker fat deposits to serve her during the long winter. Not that anyone could, but if she had been hoisted on one of those expensive, registered, official scales, she would have moved the needle to over 52 pounds.

Near the middle of the bar, she stopped finning and sank ever so slightly into the top branches of the cabbage weed below her. Perfectly camouflaged with her olive-green flanks and the wavy, slightly darker bar pattern overlay, she waited, watched, and tensed just a bit...like a coiled, fishy spring ready to release.

And at precisely the right moment, the spring within her released. She lunged forward like a freight train barreling down a track and seized a fat, juicy, twenty-inch walleye swimming along, looking for its own evening meal. Her massive maw gripped the walleye mid-body, its head sticking out one side of her mouth, and the futilely flopping tail out the other side. Big Momma clamped down even tighter on her prey, and when she detected that the flopping ceased and the walleye was dead, she released her hold, slightly, deftly turned the carcass, and re-gripped it so that the head pointed toward her throat. With a gulping motion, she swallowed her supper. As she worked the walleye farther down her throat toward her stomach with its powerful digestive juices, she finned her way around and turned toward the deep water that was always her ultimate, unseen sanctuary. A flick of her big tail, and the giant musky shot downward to digest and rest.

It was good to be the apex predator of the lake. It was even better to have learned to avoid phonies with dangling sets of treble hooks.

She was never caught.

The End

EPILOGUE

From my perspective as the author, this novella is a murder mystery set in a fish story scene that mirrors the years I spent chasing *Esox masquinongy* myself as a wannabe musky fisherman in the North Woods of Wisconsin. (Averaging once a season that I managed to put a legal-sized musky in my boat. See the back cover!)

But as was the case with previous novellas, *Cellaring* and *Death in the Dinner Group, Murder and Big Momma* is also about a very real, mostly overlooked, ignored, often denied, and very much under-funded pandemic that is even more long-lasting and widespread than the Covid-19 coronavirus that was raging as this story was being written.

The real pandemic to which I refer is most certainly woven into the very DNA of humanity - mental health issues, mental disorders, mental illness, and ubiquitous mental distress.

As cited in those previous novellas, each of which is a "stand alone" story, **mental disorders** are far more common, debilitating, and destructive than the vast majority of human beings can comprehend. The World Health Organization reasonably estimated in a recent year that **depression** affects about 300 million people at any one time. **Bipolar disorder** affects about 60 million, **dementia** about 50 million, **schizophrenia** and other psychoses some 23 million globally. And the stigma, discrimination, shaming, social exclusion, harassment, persecution, and even terrorizing and death/murder at the hands of others tremendously intensifies these mental problems. And it bears repeating from those previous novellas that when one includes individual persons, families, clans, neighbors, tribes, friends, coworkers, and acquaintances, undoubtedly 100% of humanity is touched and affected by mental disorders and mental health issues.

Every person alive on Planet Earth experiences some mental health difficulty at some point, or even every point, of their lives. The extremely vast majority are never diagnosed, never treated, never acknowledged, and certainly never accepted...whether by victim or by others, even those closest to him, her, them.

In 2013, the American Psychiatric Association (APA) defined mental disorders as "a syndrome characterized by clinically significant disturbance in an individual's cognition, emotion regulation, or behavior that reflects a dysfunction in the psychological, biological, or developmental processes underlying mental functioning." (*Diagnostic and Statistical Manual of Mental Disorders, 5th edition*) In more simple, perhaps less technical, or specialized, language, mental disorders negatively affecting, limiting, impairing, and sometimes even destroying people's lives amount to an ongoing, never-ending **mental health crisis** all around the world. Which is why I insist upon calling it a pandemic, an epidemic that affects "all people." In no way making light of the recent Covid-19 coronavirus affliction, at some point it will leave most people and countries.

Some pandemics get treated and are reduced to very limited cases. In 2018, for example, there were only 33 cases of "wild" polio and 104 cases of vaccine-derived polio recorded in the world, and only in Afghanistan and Pakistan, despite poliomyelitis having existed for thousands of years. The mental health/disorder crisis continues and will continue to plague many millions.

The fictional characters I fabricated for the purpose of this novella each and all exhibit thoughts, words and behaviors that could be expressions of mental health disorders. I do not presume, nor am I qualified, to construct depictions that accurately illustrate just how real persons exhibit such disorders. That would be the purview of mental health professionals like psychiatrists.

Nonetheless, Andy Nash, that "Paul Bunyan of professional musky guides," could conceivably be expressing *hyper competitiveness*, being extremely, even excessively competitive. Hyper-competitiveness at least resembles a diagnosable mental disorder, possibly involving obsessive compulsiveness, neurosis, even narcissism. It is sometimes referred to as **competitive disorder**.

Johnny Jenkins, the diminutive, elderly, "banty rooster" at the Guides Table, exhibited aggressiveness, very possibly dementia, perhaps related to his aging process, and possibly a mental disorder identified as **grandiose delusions**, an unusual belief about his greatness and exalted status, among others.

Sven Karlsson, the dour, usually reserved Swede, was written in such a way that he exhibited a persistent feeling of insecurity, frequently nagging worries, even envy and fears whether justified or contrived, that could suggest **delusional jealousy**. Or at least **anxiety disorder** that displays in more than 3 million cases per year in the United States alone. Symptoms typically include stress that's out of proportion to the actual impact of events, an inability to set aside worry, a restlessness of mind, body, and psyche.

157

Christine O'Malley - and don't call her "token" - could possibly be seen as developing **bipolar disorder**. Probably all human beings are subject to "mood swings," or in common parlance, "some days are good, some not so good." Every life will experience ups and downs in thinking and emotions. But those with a diagnosable bipolar disorder will experience periods of depression and abnormally "elevated" moods - the former often including fits of crying and irritability, anxiety, and exaggerated fears, the latter when they are unusually energetic and happy, or manic.

And finally, Emerson Winthrop Adams, III, was conceived of as exhibiting **narcissistic personality disorder**, possessing an exaggerated sense of self-importance, a sense of entitlement, and a constant need for excessive admiration, praise, and deference from others. His obsessive assumption of status and privilege included a capacity for rage and lust for revenge when felt as though he was wronged or denied his "due."

With a sincere apology for any inaccuracy or mistake in these fictional depictions and the suggested possible mental disorders, the concluding point this author would like to offer is that you, dear reader, and I are apt to encounter individuals like those anywhere and at any time in our daily lives, work, and "play."

Which is not to say, by any means, that healthy competition is a bad thing. On the contrary, a positive competitiveness can encourage improvement, advances, innovation, and heightened performance in all kinds of human endeavors. At least occasionally, we have to deal with individuals who are truly hypercompetitive, who become overwhelmed with their competitive efforts, and it becomes damaging to both themselves and to others.

Likewise, just because a person acts a bit curmudgeonly, grumpy, or presumes a bit of personal "grandeur," does not necessarily mean that the person suffers from grandiose delusions, dementia, or some diagnosable mental disorder.

But they may.

And it's frankly human to feel emotions like jealousy, envy, worry, and sometimes to feel insecure. Once again it can come down to a matter of degree and severity, and whether the thoughts and feelings are so deep-seated and disabling as to do genuine harm to that person and possibly others.

I have known, liked, and respected persons in my life, studies, work, and even long-term relationships who were genuinely bipolar. The ones I knew underwent diagnosis, treatment, prescribed medications, and psychotherapy. But it was always challenging, not easy to live and deal with, and somewhat perplexing to someone like me who saw the intelligence, ability, and blessings the bipolar person had to offer to others.

And finally, there's probably a good chance that you and I have experienced someone who genuinely exhibited a narcissistic personality disorder. As I stated in a previous novella, *Death in the Dinner Group*, people who are possessed by a malignant narcissism generally don't recognize or admit that they have any disorder or mental health "issue." They lack empathy or the ability to realize or much care about the feelings, lives, or well-being of others. They invariably have an over-blown self-importance and presumption of deserving praise and honor from others. A number of factors make the disorder difficult to diagnose and treat with any effectiveness. I can definitely remember someone who made my life and work difficult with those symptoms.

The mental health crisis is not going away, and we encounter it constantly as part of living on Planet Earth. As has been said about numerous threats and dangers to you and me, we ignore it or deny it at our own peril. And the cost in much more than financial ways is horrendous. A global, national, and regional movement needs to be mounted, funded, and seriously supported to improve mental health and achieve equity in mental health for all people everywhere. It threatens to become a cliche, but it's true, we're all in this together, even if we don't realize it.

Do what you can.

Thank you.

About the Author

The Rev. Dr. David Q. Hall and his wife Rev. Maxine, both retired Presbyterian pastors, live with their daughters, son-in-law, grandson, and two dogs in Oceanside, California, after moving there from the Upper Midwest forest and lake country.

His parish ministry was with congregations across the country in Pennsylvania, Michigan, Iowa, Wisconsin and California, in diverse settings including metropolitan, inner city, suburban, medium-sized and small cities, small town, rural, and the North Woods.

While pastoring a small North Woods congregation in Northern Wisconsin, Dr. Hall, a lifelong angler, fell under the spell of chasing after *Esox masquinongy*, the muskellunge or "Musky."

When questioned about the photo on the back cover of this book, he was all-too-typically vague in his answers.

"How big?" - "More than big enough." "Where'd ja catch it?" - "In a lake."

(Who's he trying to kid? We happen to know that it was 42 inches, 18 pounds. He caught it in Papoose Lake. And he's excessively proud of his *Sports Afield* "Distinguished Angler" award...but it was *thirty-five years ago*. Talk about living on past glory. Geez.)

More Books by this Author
(as of July, 2024)

Murder Mysteries

Death Most Unholy Series
Death Comes to the Rector (2017)
Death Crashes the Wedding (2019)
Death Stalks the Forest (2020)
Death Not Investigated (2021)
Death Most Unholy (next in series, not yet published)

Psychological Thrillers
Cellaring (2020)
Bodegando (Spanish version of *Cellaring* 2020)
Swarm (2022)
Death in the Dinner Group (2022)

For Younger Readers

Native American Legends Series

The Brave Birch / El Abedul Valiente
(English/Spanish 2021)
When the Owl Calls for You / Cuando el Búho Te Llama (English/Spanish 2021)
Bee Tree Honey & The Old Man and the Lynx /Miel del Árbol de las Abejas & El Viejo y el Lince
(English/Spanish 2021)
The Legend of the Niags (2021)
Brave Hawk, Crane & Pierre (2021)
Woven Native American Legends (2021)